WHAT BOOKS PRESS

AN IMPRINT OF

THE GLASS TABLE

COLLECTIVE

LOS ANGELES

ALSO BY STEPHEN COOPER

Perspectives on John Huston, ed.

John Fante: A Critical Gathering, coedited with David Fine

Full of Life: A Biography of John Fante

The John Fante Reader, ed.

John Fante's *The Big Hunger: Stories 1932 - 1959*, ed.

Struggle: The Life and Lost Art of Szukalski, Netflix Original Documentary
cowritten and produced with Irek Dobrowolski

John Fante's ASK THE DUST: A Joining of Voices and Views,
coedited with Clorinda Donato

RIVER OF ANGELS

RIVER OF ANGELS

STORIES

STEPHEN COOPER

WHAT BOOKS PRESS

LOS ANGELES

Library of Congress Cataloging-in-Publication Data

Names: Cooper, Stephen, author
Title: River of angels : stories / Stephen Cooper.
Description: Los Angeles : What Books Press, 2025. | Summary: "Mothers and
    fathers, sons and daughters, husbands, wives, and roving agents of chaos
    collide here with sometimes comic, often tragic but always lasting
    effects, against the polychromatic backdrop of greater Los Angeles: from
    a hidden wartime bunker and seedy skid-row hellhole to a grade-school
    playground, a studio soundstage, and a resplendent hilltop mansion, from
    desert to mountains to sea. These are stories of people scrambling to
    reckon with the hands they're dealt in the American gamble of their
    lives"-- Provided by publisher.
Identifiers: LCCN 2025032676 | ISBN 9798998905513 paperback
Subjects: LCSH: Los Angeles (Calif.)--Fiction | LCGFT: Short stories
Classification: LCC PS3603.O582989 R58 2026 | DDC 813/.6--dc23/eng/20250725
LC record available at https://lccn.loc.gov/2025032676

Cover art: Gronk, *Untitled*, mixed media on paper, 2024
Book design by ash good, www.ashgood.com

What Books Press
363 South Topanga Canyon Boulevard
Topanga, CA 90290

WHATBOOKSPRESS.COM

In Memoriam

Joseph Stephen Novis

son, brother, husband, father

1924 – 1958

For Janet

"You think you are lost, but it is not so, for the spirits of light will help you and bear you up in spite of yourself and beyond all opposition you may offer."

—Malcolm Lowry, *Under the Volcano*

CONTENTS

TERMINAL ISLAND

ON THE FRIDAY after the pre-induction letter came I drove my mother down to Long Beach. She had to see the doctor about her eyes, which were going bad. She had been going every week, though it didn't seem to be helping much. I would wait in the waiting room to drive her home. The waiting room was always full of old people who wore dark glasses and held on to their canes. I would skim magazines or nod off if I was loaded.

I wasn't loaded though on this day. I'd been staying straight since getting that letter. I didn't want to show up for my army physical all loaded out. So I found a *National Geographic* with a colored map folded up inside. The map went with an article about this country up in some mountains. The old men there marked their birthdays riding horses through the fields. You could see how fast they galloped by the way the pictures blurred away. These people lived to be a hundred and ten or even twenty and they took great pride in riding as fast or even faster than when they were young.

I was turning the page to read to the end when the door to the waiting room eased open. My mother was feeling her way out along the jamb with both hands. She had skin-tone patches over both her eyes held down with perforated tape. I put the magazine down and gave her my arm to guide her out.

"You get her home and draw those drapes," the doctor said from behind the reception counter.

He was shuffling papers, not even looking out through the glass partition. He was a credit doctor and he worked fast, through lots of patients, in and out. Most of his patients were old. But my mother was still young, only forty-two that summer, even if she was a widow with only one son left, and failing eyes.

"Your hand's so cold," my mother said.

I got her around the plants and the jutting canes and the coffee table, then down the cement stairs outside, one at a time. Out in the parking lot the wind was kicking papers and rocking an empty half-pint back and forth.

"You know what they say about cold hands," she said. She drew her legs inside the car. "My, but it's boiling in here."

We drove then for a while without her talking, which was strange. She usually talked an awful lot with those patches on her eyes. She would talk about the weekend, or the weather, or her book collection of Blue Chip Stamps and the new mixing bowl or maybe even that toaster she might get next time she redeemed them, anything, just to keep from saying nothing. And when we got home I would draw the shades and let her rest. The doctor was putting drops in her eyes which he said might make them burn. But she never said a word about the burning, then or after.

At the railroad crossing near the Edison plant we had to stop for the flashing light. The bell was ringing and the arm was down but there was no train. A gust of wind hit the car broadside. You could feel it lift from the rocker panels.

My mother said, "Raise the roof back home in Texas, that old wind would. Plywood ceiling. You'd see it give, then suck away, like it was breathing."

As if to show me, she took a breath. She held it in for quite some time. When she let it out the bell was ringing and still no train.

"This wind out here, it's pretty stiff but not so gritty," she went on.

"Less dirt out here to blow," I thought to say. "All this blacktop everywhere."

The bell stopped ringing and the light turned green and the arm finally hoisted itself back up. I eased my foot back off the clutch and we crossed the tracks.

"There's plenty of dirt out here," she said. "How many thousand acres of Signal Oil?"

She must have smelled the oil fields coming up then. The road went along the fields for quite a ways with the working wells and the gumdrop tanks. The air always smelled like they had just repaved the road. Of course they hadn't repaved anything, not one crack or jagged hole. High above the refinery buildings the giant chimney flames burned slanting, pale and almost smokeless against the sky. The air around them shimmered. My mother rolled her window up and folded her hands on her flower-print dress.

"Is it true you've gone and joined up in the army?" she asked.

I hadn't told her because I didn't think she'd want to know. I had joined up on the 120-day plan 118 days before. We hit a pothole. The whole seat jerked.

"They got this program," I tried to explain.

"They got a program," she said back.

"It's this deal they got for joining. You learn a trade."

A fancy tank truck cut in front of us. We appeared in its curving, shining chrome. My mother was facing straight ahead with her face held tight that way of hers.

"I told them I want to learn a trade. They said there's no better place. Building bridges. That kind of thing."

The tank truck pulled ahead. Our reflection disappeared. I don't think I believed any more of what I was telling her than the recruiting sergeant who had told me did. He had sat there with his cigarette burning while I figured how I was going to die for joining up. But it's what he had told me and I had listened and now I was telling it to my mother. She sat there by the window taking it in behind those patches. I guess she'd heard it all before, from Pat and Jamie.

"So when's the swearing in?" she said.

"Not till next week," I said. "Monday morning is the physical. They give you time to get all ready and stuff."

We drove then for a while not talking about that or anything else. For once I wished she'd just go on the way she usually did after the eye doctor. The oil fields stretched a long distance behind the razor-top chain link, a thousand wells all pumping steady in the wind.

Finally, she raised her hands up in the air and folded them tight in front of her mouth. She held them folded there with her knuckles against her lips.

"I've got an idea," she finally said. "Let's don't go straight home just yet."

Fact was, we were already getting pretty close to the projects. I could see across the oil field to the smudged gray line of cinder block. I was pretty sure my mother knew exactly where we were.

"Your eyes don't need the rest?" I said. "You know you're supposed to rest them."

"I've got all night to rest my eyes," she said. "Don't you feel like going someplace different for a change?"

"Sure," I said. How could I blame her? There were just the shades to draw at home. "We go straight home all the time. Today we'll go someplace different."

"So where do you want to go?" she said. "Is it your pick or mine?"

"Anywhere," I said.

"Then let's get away from these fields. Too much of that tar smell and you just can't think straight. We'll go someplace with a view, as dumb as it sounds."

So I turned around and drove us past the last of the Signal fields. The smell thinned down in the gusty heat. Sidewalks reappeared with walking people. There were discount houses and barbershops and places that would cash your paycheck with no ID. We passed the shot-up arrow pointing out to the prison on Terminal Island.

"That's better," she said. "I know. Let's drive up the hills there in Palos Verdes, past where all the rich people live. I'll show you a special spot I used to know." She sounded better, not so tight or now-or-never.

"A special place for what?" I said.

"Where you can see across to Catalina," she said. "Clear to the world-famous Avalon Ballroom. They turn those lights on and when the night's clear you can really see it."

I said, "Fine." The Avalon Ballroom was where you sailed across to dance cheek-to-cheek. It was one of those places from back in the old days, nothing I cared enough about to see its lights. And Catalina was just an island. Nothing special. But I was doing this for my mother, what little I could do, her youngest son. I turned off the boulevard up the winding hill toward Palos Verdes.

The commercial district fell behind and the air turned sweet with eucalyptus. The open hillsides were gold and yellow in the slanting light. We passed some stables and a tile fountain misting rainbows in the wind. I realized how often I must have driven past that fountain and never seen it. My last year in school I would drive up nights to park with girls I hardly knew, Mexican girls who kissed me back and one or two who even let me touch them, though never once did I do what I bragged of back at the projects. That was the other thing I thought would happen in the war.

The last of the guard-gate fancy houses gave way to rolling open country. We turned a curve and the ocean sparkled into view. You could see the whitecaps angling in and a big black tanker steaming south, and when I looked back down at the side of the road there was a peacock.

"We just passed a peacock," I said to my mother. I had seen peacocks at the zoo. "Standing right back there by the side of the road, up on a rock."

My mother sat forward in the seat, as if she could see its folded colors.

"Oh!" she said. "That's lucky. Was he spreading?"

I said, "It was just standing there, looking back."

"Even so," she said, "it's something. Wouldn't you say? I'd say it was."

I was glad I had told her, for it seemed to please her some way deep.

"You know my daddy kept a pair of peafowl back in Texas," she went on. "You didn't know that? Those noisy buggers. They'd keep us up nights with their singing, but he always said they were worth the trouble, just to see."

She was talking easy now, as if she had something to look forward to on the way home later on. She touched the tape around her eyes and then my shoulder with the same two fingers, then she put her arm up on the seat behind my head.

"We're getting warm now, I can tell," she said. "We're almost there."

"You'll have to tell me when," I said. "You're the one who knows the way."

"It's where I used to come out with your father back on Sunday afternoons. Back before you were born, if you can believe that. Pat and Jamie were little boys. We'd bring them along and they would play like crazy. We'd been out from Texas long enough for your dad to find some work. He was working swing there at the tire plant, six days on, Sundays off. We'd come up here different Sundays when we could. I'd pack a picnic, thick ham sandwiches and soda pop for your brothers, and chips, and Pabst Blue Ribbon beer in cans for the two of us. Ice cold. Your father would drink most of the beer himself and I'd drink a can or maybe two and the boys would play and we would take a nap out in the sun."

She leaned back against the seat with the sun now full upon her face. The sun was striking the ocean, making it shine like broken glass. My mother had never spoken much about my father or about her own life, how it was, and so it was strange to hear her talk now as we drove. My father had been killed in an accident at the Goodyear plant when I was two and when Pat and Jamie were seven and six, and she had raised us on her own there in the projects. She'd had some boyfriends but none for serious.

"Tell me when you see the lighthouse coming up," she said. "It'll be to the right, off on a point. Where the U.S. Coast Guard used to have its rifle range."

"If it's tall and white, I guess I see it," I said. "A couple miles, give or take. Though I didn't know the Coast Guard had anything these days to shoot at."

"Now find the place where the road dips down."

I slowed down so I wouldn't miss it. The lighthouse was coming up, no work to do on such a bright clear day. I started thinking my mother must be remembering things all wrong. Then the blacktop dropped from under us, sharp and sudden, so your stomach felt it.

"We're here," my mother said. "Now you can park, just anywhere. It's just a stroll to where I mean. You'll see."

I parked the car down off the road and cut the engine. It was quiet. A bird chirped off somewhere, then another, higher pitched. A whirring bug noise rose and fell upon the wind. My mother opened her door and started to get out. I went around to give her a hand.

"Now," she said. "The wire. There's still wire, isn't there?"

A three-stand fence ran between the road and an unworked field. The field sloped down toward a high curving cliff. After that the ocean stretched for miles.

"There's wire, and a little path," I said.

"You hold the wire and slip me through."

I pressed down the middle strand with my foot and held the top one with both hands. She felt for the top strand and hiked her dress and in one quick down-and-up smooth motion she was through. She stood there for a moment holding the dress up in the wind, waiting for me to climb on through the same way she had. She seemed different than I was used to seeing her back at home. She looked younger standing there with her long legs bare and that waiting look. Maybe I had never looked at her very close before, but now I did. With those patches on her eyes I could look, and I stood there looking, for a minute, maybe longer, I don't know. I think she knew what I was doing but she didn't say. She just kept standing there.

"Come on," she finally said. "We're almost there."

I climbed through the wire, nearly snagging my shirt. She let go of the hem of her dress as I stood up. The wind pressed the flower pattern against her thighs and flung her hair.

"Can you see the island?" she said.

"It's out there."

"You know that song. Let's sing that song."

She took my arm. As we walked down the brushy slope she sang that oldie, the one about sailing twenty-six miles across the waves, and all the romance over there waiting. The ocean sparkled and a rabbit jumped and a pair of quail smacked the air breaking cover, and for a time there I almost forgot about the war.

"One time," she said, "your father brought up his little .410 pump and shot a quail when it flew up in front of us. It flew right straight up in front of us and he shot it down with one good shot. But it was too little to do anything with. The boys they had to touch it and when I got it home it was just nothing, this little shot bird. He never brought his .410 with him after that."

Burrs were catching in my socks and on my mother's dress around her knees. The edge of the cliff was coming up off to the side. It curved around in a wide half-circle above the dark blue of the bay. You could hear the breakers down below and the wind.

"Now wait," my mother said.

She held me back. The edge of the cliff was still ten yards off. A wheeling seagull banked and held upon the wind.

"To the left is where it should be. Down level with the ground. It's dug in deep so they couldn't see it from on the ocean."

"Who?" I said. "See what?"

"Our place."

To the left was just more brush, a bed of cactus, a slashed-up tire, broken bottles, rusting beer cans. There was a circle of dirt with heat-cracked rocks made black by years of matchbook campfires.

"I don't see anything," I said.

"Look for concrete."

She let go of my arm. I took some steps off to the left. The seagull's shadow hung in front of me, then veered away. It crossed something light-colored, flat and solid—a slab of concrete, I finally saw. It was overgrown and almost hidden in the brush.

"You mean this thing?" I said. "This concrete slab down here?"

"You found it!" She seemed excited. "Help me over."

"Watch that cactus."

"There's a ladder in the cement we used to use."

There was an opening, four feet square, near one square corner of the slab. I kicked a tumbleweed out of the way and saw some numbers. It was a date formed in the concrete, *1942*. I leaned over the opening and saw an iron handhold leading down.

"This is it?" I said. "Your spot?"

"Not up here. Down inside. The view's in there, what you see by looking out."

I could see the space beneath the slab. It was a bunker, square and dim. There were rags and cans and bottles on the floor.

"You go down first. Then you can help me down."

She had one hand behind her head to hold her hair down in the wind. With the other she was clutching at her dress. Right then I wished we'd gone home and pulled the shades like we usually did, back to the projects where there wasn't any view. I was going off to the war and was going to end up getting killed but I didn't want to touch those rusted rungs down in that hole. Below the cliff the ocean crashed. Another stiff-winged gull streaked by. The wind felt cold even with the sun though inside my skin burned hot with fear. But it's all for her, I told myself, and clambered down.

As soon as I climbed down there it got cool and damp. I stepped off the bottom rung onto a piece of glass and felt it crack. What light there was came mostly from the slit in the seaward wall. You could see through the slit how thick the concrete was, and then the ocean, a hard bright slash.

"Okay now," my mother called. "Help me down."

She was standing at the edge of the hole in the low slab ceiling, holding her dress down against the sky. She felt forward with the toe of her sandal until it touched the edge. Then she sat down and swung her legs. She was quick even with those patches. I held her waist while she climbed the rungs down next to me. I could see what the rags were on the floor now, rotten blankets, cast-off underwear. I could barely control the trembling starting up inside.

"What is this place?" I said. "It says 1942."

My mother said, "It was for the war. The Second World one. They built these places to keep an eye out."

"An eye for what?"

"For the invasion they thought would come but never did."

She stood there just in front of me. The wind sifted in through the concrete slit. I didn't know one war from the other. She touched her throat.

"Let's go look out on the view," she said. "You can tell me what you see."

I cleared a way and walked her over. The slit ran right about the level of her eyes. A band of light cut across her face. Her hair tossed back and forth in the shining light.

"Are we there?" she said.

"We're here."

"Then tell me what you see."

I had to stoop. The light was blinding.

"Okay. I see the sky. It's really blue. There's not a cloud. And I see the ocean. Mostly ocean, no invasion. Not today."

She squeezed my hand and said, "Go on. But don't be silly. What else do you see?"

"I see Catalina," I said. "Clear as a bell and long and dark."

She stood there listening while I went on. But I wasn't looking out there anymore. I was looking at my mother, her streaming face in that band of light. In all the years I could remember I had seen her cry only twice before. Once for Pat and once for Jamie, when they were buried. They were buried a year apart but she stood there crying by each one's grave when everybody had left the V.A. cemetery but her and me. Now all I could see were those flesh-tone patches flooding tears.

"You can see it as clear as if we were almost there. By boat— by the Big White Steamship. You can see the mountains, and the town of Avalon, and I'm pretty sure you can see the Avalon Ballroom."

"Without the lights even?" my mother said. "It's not dark yet. Is it, Johnny?"

"No, it's not dark. It's awful clear."

"Oh, baby," she said. "Oh, Johnny. We made you here."

I didn't know what to make of that, or how it mattered, or if it did. But this was her day. We'd come out here instead of going home. I put my hand around her waist and kissed her eyes where they would have been and she didn't turn or take my trembling hand away. I remembered Pat then when we were young and he was the biggest, playing war, and how he and Jamie always ended up in bloody fights. I would stay quiet where I'd been killed while they would argue over whose side won and come to blows before my mother could come rushing out. She would come rushing out and pull them apart where they were rolling around in the thick green ice plant and say, "No moaning!" to whichever one was crying loudest.

The ocean echoed on the walls and the wind blew in like my brothers' ghosts. My mother kept saying, "I loved you all so much. I loved you all." Even when it got dark she kept on saying it, and when we were in the car again driving home, past the Signal fields with the giant chimneys jetting flame. The sky was orange. It rolled and pulsed, the color of night where I'd always lived. I thought of that peacock staring back at me with its feathers folded. I was going off to war. I thought I was ready for anything. I got us home and pulled the shades and started packing.

COMING OUT EMPTY

BY THIRD NIGHT'S camp they had hunted up the green canyons two mornings in a row, then late back the long way over rougher, unyielding country. But in two full days they had flushed only blue jays and one lounging marmot; and now there was nothing hanging from the deer pole.

Drew flipped his toothpick into a fire-blackened stew can.

"Not much sign even," he said. He held the mess-kit cup of coffee under his chin, staring through steam at live coals.

"Sign," said his grandfather. The steam was a blind. Pop's face sunk in the firelight. He looked thin and pessimistic. "Ain't no liver in sign."

"Five bucks they'll be moving with the snow tonight," Russell said. His speech was thick. The bottle wobbled as he passed it across the heat shimmers. "Bet?"

"You and your big imagination," Pop said.

He unscrewed the bottle cap and studied the thread. The slow-burning stump snapped and a bright swirl of sparks stuttered upward: ten billion stars swarmed the little sky visible through the lodgepole blackness above. Pop dropped the cap into the fire. It began to melt.

"Used to save this for celebrating, didn't we?"

"We'll celebrate," Drew said.

"Didn't the weatherman call for snow at these altitudes?"

"Keep talking, Russ."

"Yeah, yeah, I know. Only fools and newcomers." His voice trailed off.

Pop almost smiled. "Drink up, Drew, and we'll both miss clean in the morning. Instead of gutshooting something illegal."

Drew had had enough but he took one more last swig. "Like hell you would."

Pop got up slowly. "Like hell you say," and backed out of the firelight with the bottle. "I wonder how come it's the runt of the litter's always the hardest case."

His voice carried through the dark like a memory but Drew knew he expected no answer. It was just the damn truth. He was the hard case and Russell was the dreamer, falling asleep now in the dirt with his eyes open. His drooling big brother. When to see anything clear you had to bear down like Pop and squint. Pop went for bone whenever he could, neck shots with the least meat damage. Or shoulder: lungs-heart. Because the quicker you dropped them the less adrenaline they pumped, and the sweeter the meat. An off shot meant running them down and then gamy venison, the taste of fear on your tongue. Whereas a bullet in the brain...

Drew shut his eyes and made himself smell the raw roasting smell they needed to inhale before calling this one a trip. Their last trip maybe. If not one apiece, then at least one among them, one good buck. If only it would snow, for the tracking.

Bell sounds floated on the brittle night air. Drew got up and followed his grandfather out to where the horses stood grazing, to piss in a ribbon of starlight.

"Your back acting up?" he asked when he had emptied himself.

Pop was hunched on his heels up the low rock perch above camp where he came evenings to smoke. He would watch the creek vein through this little pocket meadow and talk Civil War stories with whoever followed him out. His own great-grandfather had fought to preserve the Union, and the stories were still fresh in Pop's mind. Now, though, he kept shifting his cigarette hand across his face, over one eye then the other.

"My back's just dandy."

"So then?"

Pop smoked some more, hacked, spit, drew deeply, exhaled.

"So try going blind and see for yourself."

Drew shook his head. "If we were all blind like you we'd have something hanging by now."

"You never know," Pop said. "Could be."

Over the frosting grass they listened to Drew's mare feed and look up, feed and look up, the bell around her neck softly chiming. This was harder than Drew had expected. Back here Pop had always worked his colorblindness to advantage, neutralizing the game's natural camouflage. Plus, he could shoot. More than once over the years Drew had seen him freeze, cheek his scarred .32-20, and squeeze one off at the blank angle of a canyon wall a hundred yards off. Or dead into alder thickets up the pumice flats from Crooked Creek. And only when the movement broke rhythm and folded into itself would Drew make out the down buck Pop had isolated from the corner of his eye. But here it was, their third night in, two more to go, and nothing was moving and nothing was hanging. *Ain't no liver in sign.*

A sharp metallic clangor untracked Drew as the stock broke from browsing and sprinted.

"That mare of yours isn't getting homesick, is she?"

Drew traced the jangling sounds within the deeper pounding of hooves to the black shape stamping the far edge of meadow. He counted four more behind, two mules, two horses, their shoes flashing silver when they kicked.

"She'll stay," Drew answered.

"Long walk back out."

"She's just stretching her legs."

"Could do with some using, don't you think?"

Drew waited for the answer.

"Tie up the mules with my horse, you and that brother of yours. That is if we're skunked again tomorrow. Then ride on up Red Slide for the night."

The chiming returned as the stock settled down. Pop took a last drag and launched the butt in a glowing arc.

"Cold camp it, like your Dad did that year."

Drew watched the glowing afterimage fade. Pop seemed to conjure one of his own.

"Perfect five-point," he said. "Thirty-seven-inch spread." He was measuring the cold with bare hands, staring at the space in between. "That ridge-running son of a bitch broke the pack-station scale, pretty near. And he never entered the jackpot."

The arc was gone.

"I thought we weren't going to talk about him."

Pop dropped his hands and shrugged.

"So I'm not the proud bastard I used to be." He reached in a coat pocket. "Here. Finish it." There was nothing in the bottle left to finish. "Just scare 'em down the mountain. I'll be waiting."

Pop raised the skin collar of his coat shuddering like a dog then straightened up tall without cursing. Pain, he had taught them, was between you and yourself. But this blind business. That was news. Or? Drew felt Pop's hand on his shoulder as the old man lowered himself off the rock.

"You know what," Pop said. His grip tightened for an instant. "You're never too old for goosebumps."

They said nothing more that night.

In the morning they wrangled under a reddening sky and the volcanic sweep of the range. But as the day wore on, broken down into vacant circles by precision crosshair optics, the world shrank to the throb of Drew's hangover; and now, with the afternoon bearing down on them, Russell was starting to grouse.

"How Winchester gets away with calling this thing a Featherlight beats the shit out of me."

The two had just converged on foot upon a high lichened bottleneck after fanning out around a broad tract of slash.

"Make a muscle why don't you," Drew said.

Russell brushed off the jibe and turned to look back.

"How far you think Pop is behind?"

Drew made sure his safety was on before slowly scoping the notch they had just worked up. Down there was nothing and nobody. And then the nape of his neck prickled up in a line that tingled and spread like hot wax.

"He's not."

"Not what?"

"Not behind us anymore."

Drew turned and shouldered and sighted on the high rock ledge at the head of the climb above them. Earlier that morning Pop had pointed it out, saying what good vantage it would be to get up that far if he wasn't so goddamned stove up.

The lens filled; and Pop lifted his trigger hand to wave across a hawk's swoop of light without disturbing the bead he had trained on Drew's heart. Drew could feel it, notched in, even as he resisted the impulse to drop. For a long moment they stood like that, each in the other's gunsight, until Drew found himself wondering if Pop had his safety on; then remembered there was none on such an antique. Drew lowered and waved back in salute.

Russell was shading his eyes with both hands. At this distance he would be able to see only the waving.

"Now how in the world did he get up there?"

"Guts," Drew stopped himself from saying, then said, "Looks like you were right after all."

A roiling continent of cloud was breasting the peaks to the west. An icy blast of wind ripped across.

"Who was it now talks weather in the back country?" Russell's eyebrows were arched. "Only fools and newcomers?"

"When you're right you're right. Enjoy it while you can. Because you and me are going up Red Slide tonight."

The grin slipped off the side of Russell's mouth. He strained to see up to where Pop had just been.

"He's not up there anymore," Drew said. "And he's not gonna be anywhere else much longer." Russell peeled his gaze from the heights to look back at Drew. "We're not coming out empty on this one, man."

Two minutes later Pop reappeared tiptoeing out from behind a lightning-struck snag. He was making antlers with his hands and dodging an imaginary fusillade. They walked back to camp without hunting.

The sun dipped away and the light turned patchy and by the time they made the lee of the ridge it was vibrant moonless night, with the storm holding off to the west. Up this high near the timberline only two twisted whitebarks managed to cling to the scree. Drew ran a picket between them and grained the horses while Russell spread the bedrolls out near the saddles. Then they ate from tin cans, beef stew and peaches, and crawled in with their clothes on, boots too. The wind came in rushes.

"Satellite," Russell said. The speck of light inched overhead, unblinking. "Like a slow-moving shooting star."

"Kind of spoils the view, don't you think?"

"What do you think Dad would say?"

Stop fighting it. Their father. Impossible not to think of him up here. Their last night in, the year it stayed summer through October and nothing was moving below, he had cold camped up Red Slide alone. The three of them had stayed behind, and the next morning Drew was the first to see him leading his horse back into camp, straight out of the sun, the great buck stretched over the stirrup leathers and the sucking sound the slit in its chest made when they shouldered it off the saddle horn.

"Remember him up after midnight?" Drew said. "Howling at the moon in the back yard?"

"*There's wolves out there in the wilderness.*"

"Way out there," Drew said. "Past the freeway."

"And those trips to the desert, chasing sidewinders."

"And the all-night boat."

"And shifting gears sitting next to him in his '52."

"Three on the tree!"

"With the naked lady inside…"

"Say it," said Drew.

"You say it."

"Okay, I'll say it. With the naked lady inside the suicide knob."

The wind had gone still. The whole sky was turning.

"Real one that time," Russell said.

Shooting star.

Silence.

And that was enough of that. Next thing they'd be saying their prayers. Their mother always said he could have gone to Annapolis if it hadn't been for the ocean inside him. He had seven tattoos, for the seven seas he liked to say, and drank bourbon-and-beer depth charges against the episodes Drew remembered hearing about through the bedroom door. Dark whispered secrets—*People grow scales and hiss*. And all the bad years, when a deer hanging in October worked as some sort of wedge against the other eleven months. The healing powers of killing deep in the forest primeval. Mother Nature, so called. When their own mother didn't stick around to witness his final slide into—the doctors had a name for it. Telling your father not to cry. It's gonna be all right. And then one clear windy night during kite season, and a single hand-loaded bullet. They never recovered the slug from the attic. Pop spackled the ceiling and painted it over. When only last year the four of them had made it up here together.

"You think we're making a mistake, Drew?"

"Doing what."

"Pretending nothing's different."

"Who's pretending?"

Drew shifted in his bag, searching out the right rocks for his bones. "Besides, what else can a poor orphan do?"

He could sense Russell timing himself. "What do you think you'll do with the insurance money?"

"Well," Drew said, "I'll be twenty-one, won't I? So why not just take that certified check and light up a big green cigar, right there in the State Farm office. Then move up here and we can talk on the phone, come Christmas."

"Goddamnit, Drew."

"And how about you—wait, lemme guess. You're going to get yourself a higher education."

"I've been thinking of it. Maybe."

"Well, *prosit*. Your ticket to the future. Does that thing go off when you want it to?"

"Come on, man."

"Set it for four."

"Drew."

"Go to sleep."

"I love you."

The wind rose back an octave higher and when they woke to the small travel alarm they were covered with a perfect layer of snow. The wind had died again, leaving a heavy brainlike sky to muffle the cold, and nothing to hear but their own movements. They shook off their bedrolls, unsheathed the rifles, and worked across the soft powder to a low scrub bank where they could crouch and wait for their chance.

When it came, they had shooting light and a wary line of deer silhouetting up the ridgeline until there were seven in all, four doe, three fawns picking their way across the smooth whiteness. They waited until the last one was gone, a whole freezing hour and no buck ever showing. When they reached the spine of the ridge, there was nothing to see on the other side but tracks in the snow and more snow without tracks, white in every direction. They saddled and headed back down for camp.

"You mind," Russell called, "if I sing a little something now that we're almost there?"

Drew turned to say yes and the concussion came up from the seat of his saddle, the sharp whiplike crack of the .30-20. And again, his mare dancing sideways, a second shot. He leaned into the tossing mane, dug his heels in her flanks, and careened into camp on a cloud of white crystals that settled hissing over a small fire. Pop was sitting on a log looking down. Drew saw he was shaking.

"I shot high," Pop said. "His rack splintered, then I hit him, my second shot. But he kept going."

He was clutching the blue octagonal barrel as if to steady himself.

"There I am picking Spam out of my false teeth and they nearly run me over. Him and his partner. Just as big."

He was pale and shaking and deeply humiliated, looking at the ground in front of him.

"I think I busted an ankle starting after him."

When Russell arrived, they got Pop's boot off and bandaged the ankle, which was already swelling. Then Drew took off in the direction Pop pointed.

He followed without difficulty through the sagebrush, though there was little blood in the snow. The deer had not taken the bullet anywhere immediately vital but he was dragging himself on his belly. Only two hoofprints showed, splayed out from the main body track and flailing. Drew climbed fast, his eyes on the spoor. He wanted to be done with this.

Ordering himself, he emptied his eyes of everything but this fitful ascent through broken snow with vivid red flecks at the edges. The buck's path of flight was direct, straight up the sidehill, away from the noise and the pain. But the pain and the noise were inside him now, and the mountain was steep, and when Drew paused to breathe and looked up, the buck stood gazing down at him strangely whole from across a rising expanse of air.

Drew thumbed off the safety and cross-haired his shot. With the recoil he felt the deer's knees buckle just as the brush before him erupted and Pop's wounded buck burst from cover, dragging itself by the forelegs. There was a jagged red hole in its spine and through the ringing in his ears Drew could hear the animal bleating.

Drew ran, dropping his rifle, and threw himself onto the bristling muscled fur, hands pressed around its neck and stabbing himself on the points not shot off, but the deer kept dragging them both higher. Its eyes were black and terrible against the hot snow as it lunged and faltered and lunged again; and when the bleating stopped inside his grip Drew had to force himself to let go. The deer's brownness smelled as his father once had. The snow turned cold again.

When he skidded it down to camp Drew told them he had missed an impossible long shot at the one's partner.

Pop said, "Never known a heart-shot animal cover so much ground."

"He's a beauty," Russell said.

"Must have been branches you saw splintering."

"Must have been," Pop said. "Must have been."

They dressed out the carcass and hoisted it on the deer pole, where it swung in the light slowly icing. Russell sliced up a fat brown onion and fried it with the liver over a smokeless fire; and though Drew nearly gagged, Pop never said a word about its un-run sweetness. What with his ankle looking bad and nothing left to drink, they decided they could pull out a day early. They had something hanging, after all.

Drew drowned the fire with water from the creek, letting the ashy river of steam wash up over him. Then they packed up in a hurry, hitching the buck across Drew's lead mule. All the way out they rode in file and talked of nothing closer to home than Civil War history and traffic.

ISAAC BABEL

IN THE SUMMER OF 197-, after a fugitive year overseas—
Åland, Ios, Lamu, Catalina—I found myself back in Los
Angeles. I was broke and nameless and starving for life. My
friend Den Gillis, a working screenwriter, took me in.

Den lived off the Pasadena Arroyo in a house filled with
books. A few years earlier he had had a lucrative run of feature
development deals, none of which survived to the screen.
Lately, to pay for his wife's treatment in a private sanitarium
back east, he'd been churning out tv scripts for a couple of cop
and detective shows.

Den had never been a cop or a detective, but now his
days were consumed with plotting out telegenic crimes and
last-minute resolutions. Nights were for drinking, watching
baseball, and talking writers. Den was a serious reader—about
his own writing he held few illusions. Except for me and my
dented Olivetti Lettera, the only other presence in that house
was the memory of Den's wife Finn, short for Philomene, a
revenant force that could lay Den low for days.

Then, sometimes, if I sensed one of his spells coming on, I would tempt fate double-clutching my way downtown to loiter along Broadway or Main to the corner of Fifth and Los Angeles, where you could forget your cares swapping lies with the other lost souls in that glorious skid-row hellhole, the King Edward Saloon.

But Den had it worse. He had watched Finn lose her starburst ingénue's mind and now all he seemed to expect from life was a back bent double to the whims of the Industry and an unending spool of misery. Still, he encouraged me.

In June, for example, he persuaded an art director acquaintance from the American Film Institute to offer me a job hauling props. The show was non-union, cash in hand every day, plus the set, this guy promised, would be swarming with women.

I turned him down.

I was hardly twenty-three but already I knew, better go hungry, or to jail, or out on the streets than to settle for less than your own way. Deep inside it pleased me to see my father, and his father, and his father before him setting their jaws in approval. Workers, fighters, drinkers, rogues—I meant to extend the line.

Den's head bobbed back and forth as he listened to me rant, his eyes brimming with bliss and dread.

In July my luck took an only-in-L.A. swerve. Den's agent knew an agent who knew a manager who had a client, Sonny Almelah, a bona fide Movie-of-the-Week mogul. Almelah's stay-at-home wife was said to be dying to make films of her own, not small-screen ephemera but quality theatrical releases—adaptations, no less, of the stories of Isaac Babel. This was a rumor that enflamed me, made my chest ache for the chance. Babel was one of those writers Den had gotten me crazy for—George Borrow, Knut Hamsun, Malcolm Lowry, the Bowleses—and now he was recommending me to help Alana Almelah launch this irresistible dream. He made a phone call. I got the interview.

The next day, sporting one of Den's roomy houndstooths, I took off across town for the Almelahs'. The address was on Cliffside at the tip of Point Dume, a blinding bluff-top pile overlooking the bay. There was a gate and an intercom and a long curving driveway, and when I stepped out of the car at the top of the crest a gust of brine filled my lungs.

"Henry Miller," I said, "pray for me," and rang the seashell door chime.

A fair-haired Mexican maid in a fitted smock ushered me in.

Everywhere I looked glass walls glimmered behind bright frameless canvases that seemed to float in mid-air. The *rubia* too seemed to float as she walked, and with that eye of hers—it was lazy, that was the thing—I thought she must like looking back when she screwed.

She left me in the living room to ponder my sins for a minute before another woman glided in. This one's hair shined dark like her eyes and the way she moved was a study. And why not? Alana Almelah was one of those wives, no longer thirty, poised between the firmness of youth and surrender to a softer age. Since Bible times, her walk seemed to say, such women have satisfied husbands who take pleasure in showing off their worth in so much ripe supple olive-green flesh.

She pressed my hands between jeweled fingers and I swear to God said, "Isaac Babel is my greatest love!"

The story she wanted to start on was "Guy de Maupassant." In fact, she had already begun a treatment, there it was right in front of me, typed pages strewn across a buttery divan.

She hovered while I skimmed. My aim was to discover if the manuscript held anything for me—nor was I disappointed. Babel's style, as sharp as whetted steel, had been dulled to crumpled tinfoil. Here was a woman who wrote like a schoolgirl practicing her penmanship. I pictured her biting her tongue, squinting to stay inside the lines, a member of that vast legion of readers with taste but no talent.

I folded the pages, promised to return the next day, and barreled back to Pasadena.

"Well," Den said when I showed him the job, "roll over, Billy Wilder, and welcome to the monkey house." He waited for me to make the connections. Then, in charity, "Okay then, go on, get upstairs and hit it."

Dawn was seeping through the curtains by the time I finished breathing life into Alana's efforts. The work wasn't as bad as it might seem. When a story is born, as Babel tells us, it is both good and bad. But there is a secret way to success. Between one's fingers the key must be warmed, then turned once and only once...

I turned the key and fell asleep, soaring.

Later that day I returned with my revisions. Alana's belief in Babel's potential for cinematic greatness was coming true, she was certain. As I read aloud what I had written she sat forward rubbing her shoulders, mouthing phrases. A mottled flush rose upon her throat.

"Where did you learn to do this?"

I told her about how writers read, about living inside the story like a sniper, or a spy, until you have transformed its secrets into your own. My hands were cold. An icy finger on her heart might have driven home the point but she kept me reading, it was clear, to prolong the moment. Her lips were glossy, parted, trembling, her hair caught sparks of light, and her legs, singing arias of the deepest belief, kept crossing higher and higher.

La rubia, looking away, appeared with our lunch.

The sovereign sunlight of Los Angeles streamed in through the window, warming the carpet, the sofa, my knees. On the table before us lay Babel's *You Must Know Everything*. One ray crept over the rough-cut edges of the volume—a sleeping volcano of human savagery and desire.

We sipped lemon water from cut crystal and set to work. "My First Fee" came next, Babel's turn on the classic boy-to-man tale, though the lusty Vera of the pointed nipples ends by calling our hero her little sister. Little sister—ha! For the shameless love-struck writer-to-be learns the seductive cunning of story, mesmerizing the wench with words stolen from novels until *she* pays *him* for his innocence.

I returned to Pasadena with Alana's down payment, a personal check for one thousand dollars. That night Den and I knocked off half a bottle of rum, chasing it with cold beer after beer. I barbecued a sagging pair of rib eyes, exhorting Den to clean his plate, then fell to railing against the disastrous theory of the auteur.

"Orson Welles? That mountebank? If it hadn't been for—for—"

"Herman J. Mankiewicz," Den said.

"—if it hadn't been for Herman J. Mankiewicz, the old fat man would still be doing parlor tricks for a living instead of flogging rotgut wine on TV."

The meat was doing its work. Color was returning to Den's cheeks, though you could still see the darting in his eyes.

"Don't move," he said, and lurched up the stairs.

When he came back down, he was clutching a pillow to his Pendleton. I thought he was going to curl up and crash but no, he pulled off the slip to thrust the ticking in my face. I backed away but he kept pressing, making sure I saw the scabby encrustations and smelled the fetid stale-spit stench.

"Get it?" Den said. "You see what I'm saying? She'd start and she couldn't stop, all day and all night. Scratching, till everything was blood."

I passed out on the couch into a brutal dream. Before Finn had suffered her breakdown I had hardly known her, and then only in a young-writer-coming-to-visit-older-writer kind of way, with Finn the demure wife making herself small in the background. Since moving into the house I had seen her likeness only once, when I turned over one of the framed photos that Den now kept face-down in every room. But for the rest of that night, in a dream that kept repeating, Finn and I devoured each other like cannibals.

In the morning I drifted into the kitchen, head pounding. Den was already at the table, bent over the National League box scores. He sat nursing a 16-ounce can of Lite, just another fan whose bride had earned an Oscar nomination for her debut film performance then plunged into irreversible despair.

Den looked up, his face a ruin, and forced a smile.

"My Cubbies," he said. "God love 'em all the way to the grave."

After that I took my breakfasts at the Almelahs', huevos rancheros, pan dulce, and enough strong Mexican coffee to power me through the day's work. By then I'd had the clutch in my car repaired, but at the end of any shift Alana might insist we cool down by taking her canary-yellow 450-SL convertible up the coast. I would steer us past Zuma and Trancas and the Navy's missile warfare station at Point Mugu and she would ask me to tell her about how I had grown up. I didn't want to do that but she persisted. Even without certain details the story that emerged was strange and mournful. I kept my eyes on the road, the grip of her attention like the aura before a migraine, and below the highway the pitiless rolling of the swells.

Eventually Alana introduced me to her husband, a bullet-headed manic who worked out in his office-gym and was forever flexing, even in his cufflinks. People whispered about his family ties to the Shah of Iran, maybe even SAVAK. The man's fortune—founded on his invention of the world's first quick-stop lube-and-oil franchise and parlayed into an empire of television melodrama—had left him with an expression of permanent giddiness. Only later did I realize how badly he embarrassed Alana.

Near the end of summer Alana's sisters—she was the middle of three—drove up with their husbands from Newport and La Jolla, respectively. The visit cost us a whole week of work. We had broken off in the middle of "The Kiss," but I kept at it on my own, and when I was finished I brought the script over early one evening. The lazy eye of the blond maid said to wait while she announced me. From another room came brassy laughter, the men's in bursts, the women's tinkling. Alana appeared in something shimmery and strapless, wobbling on ankle-ribbon espadrilles, chunky bracelets flashing silver and gold.

"Why there you are, you, you—"

She raised an imaginary glass, hitched her shoulders and fanned her hair, then did a little sideways step before collapsing upon a pharaonic settee. Beneath the shadow of her collarbone pulsed a vein.

More bursting, tinkling laughter gave way to her husband's entrance with the others, all primed for a night on the town.

Like Alana, both her sisters ferried their breasts before them, pampered women of a perilous age born to carry on the banter while their husbands patted pockets for matches and keys. They were almost out the door, on their way to the Palm and a private screening, when Alana suffered a sudden change of heart.

"I want my work to live!" she cried and sent the others on without her, the five protesting to no avail. One more group laugh to convince themselves, and they were gone.

A moment later she had me uncorking a dusty bottle and filling two chiseled goblets.

"Clos du Val '72," she said. "Worth dying for if Sonny discovers us."

But the discovery was mine, first one glass then another.

The toasts to life sailed back and forth like battlefield volleys even as a flickering alcove drew us in.

"So, now, where did we leave off?" Alana asked.

"'The Kiss'?" It wasn't a question.

"I love when you remind me where we are."

It was August in Babel's story and the war was veering around. The Poles have taken the town of Budziatycze but the Red Cavalry have won it back, raking the line with machinegun fire from careening *tachankas*. Billeted in the home of the village schoolmaster, war correspondent Kiril Vasilyevich Lyutov finds himself enchanted by the old man's daughter.

She's game, Lyutov's orderly muses, she just can't bring herself to say so.

And yet, her housedress clinging, Elizaveta Alekseyevna looks at Lyutov with eyes made bright by the hope that he will take her away to another life in Moscow.

One flaming evening Lyutov's orderly drives them in a wicker horse cart up the hill to an abandoned castle. Amidst the rubble Lyutov pulls Elizaveta Alekseyevna toward him. Uncertain and confused, she flees. Later that night he slips into her room to find her reading.

No, she says, staring up at him. Darling, I beg of you, no. And embracing his head with her long bare arms she gives him a violent, silent kiss—a silence shattered by the piercing trumpet call to arms. The brigade is ordered to outflank the Poles, who have broken through again. Galloping away, Lyutov turns to see Elizaveta Alekseyevna in her batiste nightdress, lamplight bathing her nape.

I refilled our glasses and again—"To life."

"To life!"

The maid passed through the room taking her leave.

After riding without rest for a hundred kilometers, Lyutov joins the fight, which turns into a rout, and then an endless muddy retreat. Lyutov dozes in his saddle through a late summer downpour, losing all sense of time and direction. One night, quartered in a country church, he realizes he is only a nine-verst ride from Budziatycze. To leave would be desertion—his horse is a staggering ribcage—and yet off he rides. He finds Elizaveta Alekseyevna in the same sheer nightdress, and they steal off into a shed stacked with winter potatoes and beehive frames to discover where the path from the ruined castle was always leading...

Alana exhaled. She raised her glass.

"To Babel!"

"To the castle path!"

I inhaled the peppery sweetness of her breath.

"You devil you," she murmured, falling back against the wall. Her arms made a cross—all that was missing were the nails. "You're a funny one, alright."

I drained my glass. A summer night, a vintage bottle, and the shattering power of Babel's lines had so conspired that I flung the book open and declaimed:

"During the 'Social Revolution' nobody has had finer intentions than the People's Commissariat of Welfare. Its schemes

are audacious indeed. It has been entrusted with tasks of the highest importance: to produce an immediate explosion in the soul of man, to usher in by decree a reign of universal love, and to prepare citizens for a life of dignity in free communes."

"Comrade," Alana snarled, "we have our orders."

Before the others had returned I was gone from that bloated palace. Down the Coast Highway then over the freeways I veered from lane to lane, belting out an anthem that seemed to invent itself as I drove.

Den was asleep on the couch when I came in, sports section splayed over his chest. Even unconscious his face looked pained, as if he were seeing the ghost of his beloved Finn. I slipped up to my room, switched on the reading light, and opened Conquest's indispensable meditation on the Great Terror.

That night I began to learn some facts.

After dazzling revolutionary Russia with his early stories Babel had joined the Red Army's doomed invasion of Poland. His fellow troops were Jew-hating Cossacks so he adopted a Russian-sounding name in order to write what he was witnessing—men shot to meat, castrated, stomped to death—women gang raped and cut open—children starving for milk. As Stalin's madness spiraled, Babel published less and less, but even a retreat into state-sanctioned screenwriting failed to quench his need to know. Despite the obvious risks he continued visiting a certain woman, wife of the head of the NKVD, in the hope of discovering a key to the mystery— until one night he was arrested, imprisoned, tortured, and shot, his body disposed of, his writings made to vanish with his name.

I closed the book and moved barefoot to the window. Veils of mist rose from the Arroyo like souls ascending. I thought of my father, how he had died—by his own hand, alone, begging forgiveness in a note—and of myself just starting out, shivering, full of piss, almost immortal.

THE LASH OF SAINT FRANCIS

THERESA LANDRY had just finished collecting her fourth graders' end-of-day artwork when the first truckload of Ferris wheel parts rumbled onto the grounds of Lamb of God. She stepped over to the windows and drew up the blinds.

"Class," she announced, "the fall carnival!"

Eyes widened, necks craned. Near the back of the room two boys climbed up on their desk seats.

"Rashid," Theresa said. "Jarome?"

"Day-umn," the one named Jarome said, giggling. "Ah see London, Ah see France."

He slapped fives with Rashid, who was pointing out the window at the next semi-truck lumbering past. Painted on its side a veiled harem girl struck a pose astride a prancing unicorn. Through the veil could be seen a faint suggestion of nipples.

Theresa was about to lower the blinds when she noticed the driver. He was leaning out of the cab on a ropy tattooed bicep, grinning back at the boys and gunning his engine. When his eyes met Theresa's the truck's airhorn sounded.

"*Class,*" said Theresa, but no one was listening. Still standing on his desk seat Jarome turned away, wrapped his arms around his neck, and began petting his skinny shoulders. A jolt of merriment seized the boys. The girls looked on, glances darting.

"Gentlemen," Theresa said. "If you please?"

She was nerving herself to stalk over and pull them down by the waist when the last bell of the school day jangled. The two boys jumped from their perches kicking the air ninja-style amidst much backpack zipping and snapping.

"Traffic cones!" Theresa called out. "We must stay inside the lines!"

Outside, another truck was humping over the curb into the fenced blacktop schoolyard. More trucks were lined up behind.

"And we must O-B-E-Y all safety monitors!"

Touching a forefinger to her lips Theresa held the children in place for a silent count of three.

"I look forward to enjoying these."

She raised the sheaf of self-portraits as if to inhale a rare fragrance, then smiled and nodded. Class dismissed.

Jarome was following Rashid out the door when Theresa thought to follow through.

"Jarome Evers," she said. Rashid kept going. "What do you have to say?"

Jarome swiped a knuckle under his nose, scuffed the toe of an extravagant court shoe.

"You going to the carnival tomorrow night, Miss Landry?"

Theresa pursed her lips.

"You haven't been listening, have you, Jarome?"

The answer pooled in the boy's eyes.

"Yes," said Theresa, softening. "I'll be there, at the fishing booth."

"Uh huh."

"Will you come by and see me, with your family?"

The question was not quite innocent. What Theresa wanted to learn was whether Jarome's father was still in jail. The last she had heard through the school grapevine, he had been booked on charges of assault and battery upon Jarome's mother over the issue of visitation rights.

"My family like carnivals," Jarome said.

"Well, there's so much to like, isn't there?"

"Like fish too. Like catfish. Like shark."

On the topmost paper in her hand Theresa noticed Jarome's wobbly signature. At first glance she found the image that the boy had drawn vaguely unnerving. Under a fiery sun the crude figure of a man was gripping—a dog, was it? A boy? A boy down on all fours?

"Very artistic, Jarome," Theresa said.

But Jarome was now gone too; Theresa was alone; and there it was again, surfacing, the ghostliest whisper of her returning disquiet.

Slipping Jarome's drawing to the bottom of the pile Theresa sat at her desk to compose herself. Lean forward on elbows, clasp hands behind head. Inhale. Exhale. Repeat. According to the calendar-blotter beneath her chin, compliments of O'Doul and Sons Family Mortuary, tomorrow was Friday, October 4, the feast of Saint Francis. Theresa closed her eyes to perform the Calming Neck Twist.

As recently as last year, at the earliest hint of anxiety, Theresa would have recited the soothing Prayer of Saint Francis. But of late she had been scaling back her devotions. In the years since passing forty, and especially since losing her mother, praying seemed to lead only to an unwholesome place. Taking communion, she felt her pulse race. Saying the rosary, she gasped for breath. There were even times when, despite her stock of encouraging Bible quotes, Theresa found herself fearing for her faith.

Faith is the hope for things unseen had sustained her for a time, although lately she had been clinging to *Faith is a walking in darkness*. From the evening Scripture-studies class that she had taken in the parish hall from Sister Rhonda, who held a master's degree in Contemporary Spirituality, Theresa knew that faith and doubt were like the two sides of one hand begging. Keep it open and there you had it. But how?

Fortunately, Theresa's HMO internist had offered a more down-to-earth diagnosis: she was passing through a predictable life stage. For a single woman of her age and station such a phase was understandable, especially after twenty years of teaching, all the stresses and strains and frustrations.

In those years Theresa had watched the school change. Since the horrors of the clergy abuse scandal had decimated enrollments, many of the students now being admitted were not even Catholic. Their parents—Southern Baptists, AME, actual storefront evangelicals, not to mention the out-and-out unchurched—sent the children here hoping to escape the reality behind the posted warnings at the local public school. There, a mere three blocks away, metal signs affixed to the chain link fence cited criminal code prohibiting firearms on school property. At least one of those signs—Theresa saw it every afternoon driving home after work—was riddled with rusting bullet holes.

It hadn't always been so. When Theresa started teaching, there had been no homeless encampment on the other side of the storm channel adjacent to the school, no gaunt wild dogs roaming the concrete embankment, no fourth graders like Jarome with struggling single mothers and violent— imprisoned?—fathers. And that was to say nothing of the poor unhoused soul discovered one morning hanging by a length of knotted rope from the highest rung of the children's jungle gym. According to Theresa's doctor, such developments could have a negative effect on a person's outlook, and no wonder. But there were steps they could take together, as a team.

After a few weeks of pharmacological probing and two or three panic attacks, they had hit upon the right brand and dosage of antidepressant. Since then, things had improved. Theresa's moods had stabilized and the prescribed yoga poses helped. The Calming Neck Twist was particularly beneficial.

Now Theresa raised her head, centering herself before the rows of unoccupied desks, and took a final cleansing breath. Despite the occasional whisperings, she was no longer assailed by the need to pray quite so often, or so hard, or to live in mortal dread of that need. If she could help only one child each day, make a positive difference in a life—that would be her way of hoping.

An hour later, having updated attendance records and prepared tomorrow's lesson plans, Theresa gave herself over to perusing the day's art assignments.

Draw a picture of yourself for your best friend.

As always, Theresa was touched by the sincerity of expression in the broad lines and bright strokes. She was especially pleased by the details lavished on all those eyes. There were lashes and lids and irises and pupils and, in her favorites, earnest attempts at lifelike tear ducts.

"Super!" said the stickers that Theresa pressed on to the waxy colors. *"Terrific!" "Hooray!"*

Flipping to the next sheet she found herself back where she had started, with Jarome's disturbing self-portrait. Unlike all the other drawings, this one was not a close-up study of the artist's face. Instead, Jarome had sketched a manlike figure with powerful legs and arms, as if from some cautious remove. But was that a dog in the figure's clutches, or a boy? Theresa could not puzzle it out. For a moment the word *clutches* swam before her eyes.

The disquiet was a small one this time. "Go away," Theresa said without saying anything aloud; and the feeling faded into the fluorescence.

She was straightening the edges of the drawings when Hector, the school janitor, leaned in the doorway.

"*Permiso,* Miss Theresa?"

"Hello, Hector."

"Yes, Miss. But jour car."

"My car—yes?"

"*Sí, es* blocking one truck for the *carnaval.*"

Theresa thanked him and gathered her things.

Outside the classroom Theresa's breath plumed before her. She buttoned up her sweater against the uncommon chill and set out across the blacktop, cutting through a lane of orange traffic cones past piles of plywood, metal piping, and fiberglass parts being offloaded from the shabby fleet of carnival semis.

Approaching her hatchback Theresa felt a trembling in the ground beneath her feet. It was the truck with the painted harem girl looming ahead, engine idling, stake-bed trailer helter-skelter with spooled cable, riveted struts, and gaudily lettered wood panels.

"I been looking for you."

Theresa suppressed the instinct to flinch. Coming from behind her, the voice sounded dimly familiar. She fastened the last button of her sweater and turned to see a lanky blond stranger with pinpoint eyes and a jaw like the blade of a knife. It was the driver, the one who had honked at Theresa's class through the windows. The cant of his hips slowly switched.

"That your little red rocket?" the man said.

His chin lifted to indicate her car. He was rawboned and younger than Theresa by a few years, perhaps, with a mustache that failed to hide the seam of a joined harelip.

"I'm moving it," Theresa said.

"No hurry," the man said.

"It's alright. I was leaving."

"So soon?"

From denim vest to fraying boot cuffs and underslung heels the man was a carny through and through, no one Theresa had ever known in this life. And yet his voice, something about it, she seemed to recognize.

"I'm finished for the day," Theresa said.

"And here it is mine just starting up," the man said. "I mean, you know, the night."

He pulled on the mustache. Theresa turned toward her car.

"Coming back?" the man asked.

Theresa paused. "Excuse me?"

"For the rides."

Engine heat wavered above the hood of his truck. Theresa felt the urge to pray and dispelled it.

"Because you won't need no ticket to ride mine."

Theresa's head went heavy, then light. What was he saying? He was propositioning her, wasn't he? Right here on diocesan asphalt and less than a minute after they had met. But why did his voice still sound familiar, the voice of this stranger with dirty thumbnails hooked in the belt loops of dirty jeans? And why did she want to hear more of it?

Theresa said, "And what ride would that be?"

Her glance cut to the jumble of cable and stacked plywood behind the truck's pinstriped sleeper cab.

"Come back tomorrow night and see," the man said.

"*Cyclo*—"

Theresa was sounding out the fancy lettering on a sheet of paint-thickened plywood, the first part of an unfinished word.

"You know the one." The man lifted a hand and spiraled it upward. "Round and round and round she goes, where she stops—" The hand came down. "Which I could of got killed hauling it here through the damn ghetto."

Theresa winced.

"The what?"

"You heard," the man said. "Left on Florence, right on Vermont. Name of Reginald Denny ring any bells?"

Against her will Theresa's inner eye filled with the hovering news-copter view from L.A.'s last major riots, blazing palm trees, marauding thugs, the hapless teamster far below being dragged from his big rig and savaged.

She dug in her purse for her keys.

"I mean," the man went on, "you tell me where you think we are."

Theresa's answer was automatic. "We're in the playground of Lamb of God Elementary."

The carny sneered, as if the many hopscotch squares, tetherball poles, and raised beds of the children's garden all counted for nothing.

"Tell me more," he said. "Like for example which box you like to check. White, black, or indecided?"

Theresa's fingers found the keys and pressed the remote, she heard the locks in her car elevate. The man stepped sideways— was he trying to stop her?—only to open and hold the door, like some kind of gentleman in disguise. Theresa hesitated then sat down in the driver's seat, conscious of her legs and the way she drew them in.

"Okay then," the man said. "But don't you forget. You're coming back to see me, now aren't you."

It wasn't a question, and he wasn't asking.

"Cross your heart and hope to die."

"I work here," Theresa said.

"I know what you do."

For a moment he seemed to study his hand, turning it over, knuckles to palm.

"I'll be at the fishing booth," she said, filling with fear at the admission. "From six until closing time."

The man produced a smile. The hairs of his mustache stretched thinner.

"Now that's my doll now," he said.

Theresa drove through the schoolyard tingling. Just before the driveway exit she looked up in time to slam on the brakes and avoid hitting Father Ngabire. The startled missionary skipped backwards, nimble even in his cassock, while managing to hang on with both arms to a large meshwire bingo hopper. Theresa lowered her window.

"Saint Christoph-ah, protect us!" Father Ngabire cried, his great kindly red eyes rolling heavenward.

Theresa understood the joke but could not bring herself to join in.

"Although you have been disappeared," Father Ngabire continued, "dear most venerated Christoph-ah, patron saint of world travelers, watch over us on our journey wherever it may lead and keep us safe from bots out of hell like dear Miss Landry!"

Bats, Theresa thought, he means to say bats, as with a wide ivory smile Father Ngabire offered his blessing. She never saw the awful scar that creased the priest's forehead without imagining the machete that had hacked him nearly to death. A survivor of the Rwandan genocide, Father Ngabire was always eager to make people smile along with him, and Theresa usually obliged. She was one of the few parishioners who listened hard enough to understand the tortured English of his homilies as he labored to balance harrowing tales of atrocity against the mysteries of redemption with a running patter of jokes gleaned from *Our Sunday Visitor.*

"I'm sorry, Father."

"Go and sin no more," the priest chortled.

"I need to watch where I'm going."

"Yes, yes, so do we all, so do we all. But we shall see you tomorrow evening, at the fishing?"

"I'll be there, Father."

"Fine." The priest touched Theresa's arm with two tapering black fingers. "We'll see you then—the communion of saints and yo-ahs truly!" He was still chuckling as he shambled away.

Three blocks later, passing the neighboring public school, Theresa forced herself not to look aside at the shot-up sign. At home in her apartment, she drank a glass of Charles Shaw Chardonnay with her Weight Watchers Oriental Combination and another glass watching *Survivor.* The second drink was a bread substitute for the rice noodles she sucked on before removing them from her mouth with a paper napkin.

On the TV screen sweating contestants in torn shirts and bright bandanas were conniving to cheat or seduce one another in some snake-infested tropical paradise. Theresa dozed off during a sponsor's litany of possible side effects. For two hours she slept heavily and for six more she lay awake, trying not to be afraid and failing.

Driving across the storm channel overpass early the next morning Theresa saw the assembled Ferris wheel standing motionless against a streaking cirrus sky. The half-day schedule passed in a blur. Jarome was absent, and the empty seat only added to her worry, all the more so when during recess his mother did not answer Theresa's repeated phone calls. Afterward, with the carnival taking shape outside the classroom windows—spinning cups, Tilt-a-Whirl, merry-go-round, the Hammer, all going up before the distracted eyes of her children—Theresa found it impossible to hold their attention. Abandoning her lesson plan, she read aloud from *Falling Up*. No one noticed when she lost her place and read the same poem twice.

By half past eleven her head was throbbing. She took two extra-strength painkillers and then a third before declaring the rest of the morning a bonus free-drawing period. She used the time to sit at her desk performing a discreet series of Alternate Nostril Breaths, trying to balance her positive and negative energies.

Soon the Angelus was knelling under a deepening cloudbank while cars full of children processed out of the parking lot. From her vacant classroom Theresa surveyed the lines of fluttering candy-colored pennants and tarped booths, all in place for this evening's opening of the carnival.

For a moment she considered leafing through the latest batch of artwork. But Jarome's whereabouts still troubled her, and the thought of the man with the crooked mustache made her want not to be alone. She closed the room and walked down the corridor to the teachers' lounge.

Inside, the atmosphere was cramped and clammy, but a festive air obtained. Sister Rhonda had called out for pizza.

"Oh, go ahead, Theresa," said Theresa Boyle, the other Theresa of Lamb of God, when the first Theresa declined a slice. "You only live once, you know."

The first Theresa was hungry but she didn't want to eat yet.

"Sausage and onion," said Sister Rhonda.

"Mmmmm," said the other Theresa.

"Easy for you to say," said obese Rose DeForno.

"My bad?" said the other Theresa, a legginged fiend for all the girls' P.E. she taught.

"With your ribs sticking out from all that spinning?" said Rose. "Come on, Boyle, give us a break."

Theresa Landry summoned herself. "Actually," she said, "Theresa is right."

Sister Rhonda sat up in her shirtwaist. "Pray tell about what."

"We only live once."

"Bite your tongue," said Sister Rhonda.

The other Theresa held her half-eaten slice up in the air as if to trace some kind of sign.

"All I meant was have some pizza," she said. "Warm yourself up. I mean like, it's freezing out there."

For several seconds the mysterious tracing hung before the first Theresa's eyes.

Help yourself, the whispering said. *Be quiet,* Theresa told it. The others were watching her. She listened to them chewing.

"Anyway," she said.

"Anyhow," said Rose.

"Any WHO let the dogs out!" woofed skinny Theresa Boyle, shimmying in place and working the hinged cardboard box like a giant mouth.

"Thanks," Theresa said, "but I'm saving myself."

She sipped her diet soda taking care not to crunch the ice and thus reveal the swerve of her dislocation. Sister Rhonda, who was the principal, flexed an elbow.

"All this commotion," said the nun, "and now my joints are saying rain."

Rose was eyeing the last slice in the box. Despite her girth she was empty inside. Theresa could feel the void.

Later, over the heads of all the fun seekers, greasy barbecue smoke churned up into a night sky crazed with searchlights. Synthesized calliope music vied with chiming bells, ahooga horns, and the baseline thrum of diesel generators. Later still, a screaming deejay with a reverb foot pedal set to work.

Theresa sat bundled up on a folding chair behind a tarp daubed to suggest watery depths and cavorting fish. Beside her stood a bucket of clothespins and a tub filled with prizes. Glancing beneath the lower edge of the tarp Theresa could make out the shoe tips of the people who came to fish. The shoes helped her decide what kind of prizes to hand out.

A bamboo pole would poke over the top of the tarp dangling a plastic hook on a braided cord. Theresa, unseen, would look at the shoes then clip on a packet of superhero cards, or a pair of bouncing eyeball antennae, a rubber tarantula, a string of princess pearls.

She hadn't eaten anything since last night at home. Her thought was still to save herself, for later.

The first shoes that she recognized, woven loafers of a sub-Saharan cast, belonged to Father Ngabire.

"I feel a big one," came the priest's droll voice through the tarp. "A finny monst-ah!"

"*Jaws!*"

It was the other Theresa, Theresa Boyle, who even in this age of soaring clerical liabilities hardly bothered to conceal her hots for anything in a Roman collar.

Theresa attached a miniature chess set to the hook and tugged.

"Checkmate, Miss Landry!"

"Hello, Father," Theresa called.

"Please to remember to come up for air!"

Beyond the tarp Father Ngabire laughed, and so did Theresa Boyle, whose turn it was now to dangle the hook even as she teetered on trashy open-toe heels. Rummaging in the prize tub Theresa attached a flexible glow-in-the-dark slave necklace, but instead of letting go she held on. The ensuing tug-of-war ended abruptly with the braided cord snapping off in her grip.

"The one that got away!" laughed the other Theresa.

"And Saint Christoph-ah," Father Ngabire called. "Don't forget poor Saint Christoph-ah, Miss Landry!"

That was the joke: except as a figment of pious legend, Saint Christopher no longer existed. Which had never dissuaded Theresa's mother from keeping his magnetized likeness on her dashboard, or from invoking his intercession while stirring the roux, stirring and stirring, around and around, as if achieving just the right muddy shade and texture was never anything short of a miracle. The corroding automotive accessory now lay locked in Theresa's cedar hope chest, along with her mother's evil-eye gris-gris and the holy card from her funeral. The card showed the sturdy-legged Christopher fording a river, staff in hand, with the Child Savior perched high and safe on one broad shoulder.

A throaty snuffling noise made Theresa look down. The drooling muzzle of a dog was rooting under the tarp, one of the storm channel strays, no doubt. When she stooped to shoo it away she saw the scuffed toe of an extravagant court shoe.

"Jarome?" Theresa said.

Inclining her head toward the tarp Theresa felt a stab of hope.

"Yo, Miss Landry."

"You came to see me," Theresa said.

"Uh huh."

"With your family?"

"With my dog," Jarome said, "and my daddy."

"Heel."

It was a man's voice, harsh and rasping. Theresa smelled something acrid, like burning plastic.

"I said heel!"

The dog yelped and a bamboo pole angled in over the tarp. Theresa pinned a box of crayons to the hook. The prize rose on the braided cord and disappeared.

Theresa sat waiting for Jarome to say *Day-umn*, or *Thank you*, or *Goodbye*. Hearing nothing she stepped out from the booth. The boy was being led away through the crowd by his father, a wraith in a bulging hoodie holding the boy's neck in one hand and in the other a chain stretched taut to a junkyard mutt straining to sniff up every passing human leg.

And then the lightning—a single boltless flash illuminating several visitors wearing skull masks and devil faces. Or were they? Wasn't it too early for Halloween? Too soon for the Day of the Dead?

Lord, began the prayer...

The first drop of rain fell on the corner of Theresa's mouth. She licked her lip tasting what it must taste like to lick the newest street in Los Angeles, tarry and granular and unnamed. And then, trembling up from under her, the thunder.

The downpour came fast and pounding. People were covering themselves, running, splashing through puddles. Theresa walked on, soaking through. Soon all the exposed rides had stopped turning, the whirling caged things, the infernal Ferris wheel. The carnival was almost deserted and still Theresa walked, through swirling veils of rain; and when she looked up there it was, the flickering lights of the entire word.

"Cyclo-Rama-Clone," she read aloud.

It was a small hangar-like enclosure at the far end of the carnival to which Theresa was making her way through the storm.

At the top of the rubber-matted ramp, in the shadow of the entrance, the lanky blond man stood waiting. One side of his mustache twitched up.

"My favorite cinnamon girl," the man said, easing the door open without seeming to touch it. "Come on in out of that wet and get cozy."

The collar of his jacket was turned up and in the curl of his tongue was a clove, the black tip of which he let her see flicking.

"Do I know you?" Theresa asked.

The smile stretched tighter.

"Just watch that pretty little step of yours going down."

Inside, sticky stairs descended into a dim cylindrical space reeking of WD-40 and ozone. A wall of vertical staves circled all the way around, like the interior of some ancient cistern. Though she hadn't paid any admission Theresa was the only customer.

"Alrighty almighty," said the man, closing the door and approaching. He snapped his fingers and patted the air in front of Theresa's breasts until, backing away, she felt her shoulder blades touching the wall. The man patted the air one last time before sidling to the crude cockpit-like enclosure at the center of the attraction.

"Ready for blastoff!" he announced, sitting down at the control panel. He pointed at Theresa, pushed a button, and pulled a lever.

From below came a mechanical groan and shudder. The room began to rotate.

Theresa stretched out her arms to either side, opening her palms. The turning accelerated, revolution after revolution, until her whole body was pressed against the wall. She tipped her head forward, but the force of the spinning jerked it back, the floor dropped from under her feet, and an unearthly musical shrieking commenced.

Theresa was fastened to the wall circling the harelip, who sat in the still center of the room grinning serenely. The bones of Theresa's back dug into the wood, blood was rushing to her fingertips, and her panties were bunching up, higher and higher.

"Get up on it!" the carny lip synced.

Leaning away from the force of the centrifuge he rose to his feet on the lowered floor, removing one hand then the other from the controls. The angle he was standing at looked impossible to maintain but there he stood, shoulders rolling, mouthing the invisible air mike in his fist.

"Ma-ma-ma-make the scene!"

And then he was dancing toward Theresa, all slide step and groove. For a moment she squeezed her eyes but instead of darkness all she saw was a funneling prism of colors.

Lord, make me an instrument, resumed the prayer, even as the carny went on defying gravity to hover before her, his breath sweet and scorching, his eyes mirthless slits. *Make me an instrument,* said the whispering, *or go to hell.*

Theresa gasped. The gall of the demand brought back the death of her mother as if in some night-vision tableau, the crucifix on the bedstand, the vials of holy water and chrism, the delirium in her eyes as she bolted up to croak, "I know your fucking name you devil you."

In the end Theresa had prayed for death to come, not out of love, or exhaustion, but from rage at the absent God who made all things, who made horror and loss and loneliness; and then her mother had died. Ever after which to pray was to lie, and to lie was to sin, that's how it felt whenever Theresa made brave to try. And yet why did she go on trying?

With all her strength Theresa peeled her arms away from the wall for a pleading moment before they were pinned back down by the pull. Again she forced them in front of her to reach out and, what? Embrace the secret Jesus holed up in the leering carny? Touch the hem of that mended lip? All she knew was she needed to reach, and she kept reaching, and praying, if that's what it was—*"Go to hell, go to hell!"*—until the carnival man, recoiling, spidered back to the controls to hit the kill switch.

The music stopped, the spinning slowed, the floor rose back into place. All was still. Before Theresa could regain her balance, the carny was gone.

Outside, the rain had scoured the midway of carnivalgoers, strewn it with sodden cupholders, clotted hotdog buns, a filthy tube sock, shredded tickets; and beside the fishing booth, in an ankle-deep eddy of foam, something long and sinuous and struggling. A snake? A snake, could it be, that needed her?

As a girl Theresa had cared for the family snake, small and green like the green of her mother's garden, that little piece of Plaisance on St. Elmo Drive, and a joy to feel coiling around her fingers. But even a snake could drown.

She reached down into the foam to clasp the poor creature to her breast only to find herself clutching a snapped-off length—the other Theresa's?—of braided cord. Plastic hook and glowing necklace had vanished on the flood, but the cord somehow remained. She raised it to her cheek as if in gratitude. The unraveling strands, dripping and stiff, felt like the caress of some rough hand. She shuddered and drawing in a brave hopeless breath twisted the strands into a double knot.

Across the surging storm channel, a small fire burned against the underpass black of the homeless jungle. Dog shadows mingled with men's. A biting welt rose on Theresa's neck at the first kiss of the scourge. Offering up everything for Jarome, she said a prayer, turned toward the flame, and kept walking.

RIVER OF ANGELS

NIGHTS WHEN WE'RE HIGH Cui takes me down to the river. We jump the barrier, head for shadows, make love. Everything is concrete, pouring down to the channel. The water at the bottom smells black. When we rock, the mural peels, Cui's long-ago spray strokes. Paint chips stick to our bruises.

Other nights we drive out to the desert. The turnoff isn't marked but Cui knows the way. He parks where the blacktop ends. We smoke dope and doze while beyond the curve of windshield a jetliner rims the stars.

At dawn we climb out and start walking. I carry the gunnysack and Cui carries the stick, through prickly pear, greasewood, tumbleweeds, yucca—until Cui pulls up short and points.

Chingón, he says. *Señor Sidewinder.*

The tracks lead away like lazy *S*'s over the wash, disappear under a pile of rocks. Cui kneels down in the sand. He removes one rock, then another, peering in. The snake lies coiled against the chill, slow-blooded. Cui reaches in, grips the head, and lifts.

Later, under the sun, Cui goes to his stick. He's running and I'm running to keep up. He pins another, even bigger, and it's whipping something fierce while I swing the sack open to keep number one from pitching out at my jugular.

With two now inside, it's live weight I'm lugging, then another, and another, and two more.

Driving home to L.A. I keep slapping Cui's cheekbone so he doesn't nod off and veer over the stripes. In the trunk I can feel that sack just crawling.

Eighty bucks a head is what we get, going price, at the smoky Koreatown *botanica*. The venom, snake sushi, fang charms, Spanish fly: They don't waste nothing, Cui says.

Cui is a smart one, in spite of himself. Between the two of us we have our own private reading circle.

Cui brings home books that he steals from the library, mostly true-life adventures: *Lavengro, We Die Alone, The Long Walk*, etc. In *The Long Walk* these prisoners during World War Two escape a Russian death camp to spend the next year walking for their lives. They walk south from the Arctic Circle across Siberia, the Gobi Desert, over the Himalayas into India, starving and freezing and hallucinating. One of them is this innocent young Polish girl. Even though she's beautiful and the only woman in sight, nobody tries to fuck with her, and when she dies the men are stricken with grief.

I close the book and look at Cui. He's trembling, off a jag.

Different world back then, I say.

We're in bed, a grimy mattress on a sea of red linoleum. The abandoned apartment we're squatting sits under the flight pattern of Hawthorne Municipal. Every breath tastes like burning jet fuel.

In lighter moments Cui reminds me we've landed in the hometown of the Beach Boys, George Harrison's widow, the former head of the National Endowment for the Arts, not to mention near the old Holly's on Hawthorne Boulevard, site of the infamous hold-up scene in *Pulp Fiction*. But no amount of pep talk can stop the broken glass in the window frames from rattling at night in the wind. Tonight is one of those nights.

Cui holds me, kisses me, breathes warm on my breasts. I can hardly hear him when he whispers but I can read his strung-out mind.

Same world, he's thinking. Different war.

We go to Sony to hit up Cui's brother. Sure enough, the guard hassles us at the gate. The visitors list on his computer doesn't show Cui's name.

Spell it again, says the guard. From the beginning.

He's leaning down from the booth trying to see through Cui's shades, wondering if his next step should be to buzz Security.

Cabrón, Cui says to the dashboard.

Wipe the sweat off, I say.

Right, Cui says.

And be nice.

Be nice. Okay. And then, to the guard: I'll do anything for this girl so lick your pencil and listen up. C-U-I-T-L-A-H-U-A-C.

The guard is chewing his mustache, about to say Sorry, when Dex coasts up on his beach cruiser. Dex is wearing work boots, board shorts, and a t-shirt that says One God, One Country, One Fin. A paper dust mask hangs from his neck.

I'll vouch for them, Antoine, he tells the guard. Just don't ask why, okay?

Cui's eyes brighten with brother-feeling and need.

Soundstage nine, Dex says. Tallyho.

Dex is carving thunderheads. A prototype hangs above us on invisible suspension wires, enormous and swaying slightly in the conditioned air.

What's this one about, Cui asks. He means the movie Dex is working on these days.

We're walking through the vast hangar scattering Styrofoam shavings around our ankles.

Sculptor's motto, Dex says: Know the story, go to hell.

Cool aerials anyway, Cui says.

He's leafing through the cloud photos spread out on Dex's workbench. I notice Dex noticing me scratching the backs of my legs. When I stop scratching, the itch spreads like fire.

Check out this monster, Dex says.

I peer over Cui's shoulder at the glossy photo, a storm cloud straight out of Revelations. Dex carved the Lincoln Memorial in *JFK*, half the palm trees in *Cast Away*, the hideout cave in *Ironman*, etc. He's good, works fast, stays clean.

You look hungry, he says, his eyes seeking mine. Ginny looks hungry, doesn't she, bro?

Yeah? Cui says. Well, you know how it is.

We're walking under the foam cloud toward the great airy opening on the other side of the soundstage.

Sure, Dex says, I know. Real artists suffer, right? No compromises? No union perks?

He steps out into sunlight, lifts his teeshirt, pats his abs. Cui holds me back by my arm.

Stop scratching, he whispers, before you get an infection.

We catch up with Dex out in the glare.

Yo Dex-man, calls a stagehand riding toward us on a forklift. He's looking back and forth, from Dex to Cui, from Cui to Dex. How'd you ever get such a handsome twin brother?

In the studio commissary I eat as much as I can, tuna salad on a brick of lettuce, but when we're finished my plate is still full. It's like so Calling-All-Straight-Folks I can hardly pretend.

Dex palms Cui a folded hundred-dollar bill. This is exactly one-fifth of what Cui has stooped to beg for during lunch to help cover the rent as he puts it; but money's not what he needs most. Dex knows this and I know that he knows that I know, etc. It's there in his face, in the pinch of his eyebrows as he pockets his wallet and buttons the flap.

The moment is a glass bubble filled with more shame than I can bring myself to share. But I share it and smile and so does Dex as we say our goodbyes near the black iron gates out on Overland. Dex punches Cui on the shoulder, kisses me on the ear.

Don't look now, he says, tilting his head toward the vintage convertible gliding onto the lot, but there goes what's-their-name.

We're back at the river, broad daylight, breathing ozone. It's the next day, or maybe the next.

There's a half-submerged shopping cart with a bird's nest in the kid's seat. Mother bird swoops down from the sky. She's feeding her children, but with what? Glittering earthworms? Chewing gum foil?

You can stretch a hundred dollars all sorts of ways, some of them unthinkable, as when Cui strips off his shirt and wades in up to his waist though he's still wearing his slacks and huaraches.

Bird flies away but keeps dive-bombing Cui, swooping down so close that his hair twirls up from the cowlick. Not that Cui in his trance even notices. His back glows in the sunlight as he dunks his works beneath the surface and does up with oily gutter particulates.

How did we get this way? There's a reason for everything. Ours was, we wanted a fastness.

Cui taught me that word, and that for every new one you learn it's yours to recast the world with. As in, Welcome to our fastness, spreading your hands hostess-style, wherever the hell you might be. As in, I've cut ties with home to live my life with Cui and so I'm free to do as I please.

When the day comes, we make a pact. It's us against the world, is what Cui says.

He goes first and again doesn't die. A minute later I take a breath and go too.

When my eyes flutter open, there's Cui, smiling down on me like heaven's brightest angel. There we both are, together, new and shining.

Cui's art is a thing of the past. If you know where to look you can still see the stuff that hasn't been lost yet to progress, or the elements. His Histories of the Future series along the cement banks of the river. The Hieronymous Bosch triptych off the 210 near Temple City. The Belmont Tunnel extravaganza. Shake Hands with Gonga across Crenshaw from the refinery. The notorious self-portrait at Wreckerz Paradise in Wilmington, etc.

Fortunately, Cui has yet to follow through on his threat to rent a sandblaster and make an end to everything once and for all.

When a stringer for the *L.A. Weekly* appears at our motel room in Corona sniffing out a whatever-happened-to featurette, we bail for less trafficked pastures.

There isn't a bus tour yet of the remnants in all their faded glory, but I wouldn't bet against such a travesty, some day.

I go for weeks forgetting the girl I used to be. Seeing me work the offramps, darting in and out of lanes in my thrift-store parachute pants, who could imagine the onetime homecoming princess writing love letters to her assistant cross-country coach, then burning them under the ceiling fan in her grandmother's upstairs bathroom? Or the near-graduate of Long Beach State but for three idiot science credits, Studio Art major, minor in Creative Writing, poetry, feeding French fries to the pigeons in Dam Square? Or the office temp filling in for sick receptionists, dying file clerks, deported nannies?

My family doesn't count anymore. I forget them for the sake of Cui, who has convinced me that in this world each other is all we can depend on.

For one thing, he's also out there working to keep us going. Just another hungry-eyed laborer milling around outside Home Depot, flagging down sport utility vehicles for an honest day's pay—ha. When what he's really doing is casing construction sites for goods to boost on stoned midnight raids to these guys who pay cash in the hand, no questions asked, for power tools, jalousie windows, water heaters, pallets of brick, insulation, bales of wire, etc.

Even so, he still takes the time to make me a reversible cardboard sign. On one side it says *Smile! God Loves U!*, on the other *AIDS Baby at Home Mercy Please*. Both sides are decorated around the edges with the same seizure-inducing pointillism, like a comic strip seen from too close up. In fact, it's adapted from the Aborigine, the same Dreamtime design that with a little pilfered electricity Cui has begun tattooing on his own face.

Cui runs a fifty-foot extension cord out the second-floor window of our squat to the circuit box behind the body shop next door. The atavist in him keeps the guard dog from attacking.

If he can finish the pattern on his left cheek before the day shift starts arriving, we won't need the connection anymore.

He works by streetlight with the mirror propped in the sill of the kitchen window. Drops of blood seep from his jaw and run together. While he's applying the needle it hums this low steady note, and when he stands back to figure, the note rises.

By shifting his focus in the mirror, he can watch me watching him from behind.

You're beautiful, he says, chin glistening.

What he means is, You're next. That's where I draw the line.

You know, he says, you're really beautiful, and leans back into the mirror.

I can almost feel the pattern taking shape on my own cheek.

Cui brings home *Life on the Mississippi*, which turns out to be even better than *The Long Walk* and *We Die Alone* combined. We take turns reading out loud, cracking each other up.

A river runs through it all right, Cui says.

With all the maiming and murder and accidental fatality they could call it *Death on the Mississippi*.

If I had been a girl I would have cried, Cui reads.

He's speaking to the book now, cradling it like a newborn. He rips out the page with those filed teeth of his and chews it like some kind of ruminant.

We're walking east on Imperial Highway, through Athens, through Watts, carrying clothes, books, toiletries, blankets, Cui's inks, my makeup, etc., all stuffed like a body in our sleeping bag.

Seeing Cui's face, even the mumblers and stumblers outside all the liquor stores step aside.

Our car has disappeared and we've been run out of our pad by a startled city health inspector anticipating mere vermin.

I am the only white person in sight.

Walking along the cracked and dated sidewalk—*1946, 1933, 1929*, etc.—Cui says, Great rivers of the world. Go.

Between us we come up with the Nile, the Amazon, the Congo, the Colorado, the Thames, the Volga, the Mekong, the Slave, the Jordan, the Liffey, the Rhine, the Yangtze, the Tiber, the Hudson, the Snake, the Saint Lawrence, the Danube, the Seine, the Niger, the Guadalquivir, the Tigris and the Euphrates.

Where it all started, Cui says. Civilization, man, the first laws.

He's riffing now, manic.

Though where these days you can turn up floating merrily down the stream without your head. Decapitated! And speaking of Hawthorne, he continues, Nathaniel now, dig it, don't forget how he helped haul the maiden corpse of that chick up from the Merrimack. The marble hardness of her arms? The gore streaming from her nose?

So much for this world, we agree. We pass a homemade bus bench memorial though who died it doesn't say, plastic flowers, melted votive candles, laminated placemat Sacred Heart.

Which leaves us with what, Cui says. The Los Angeles? The Styx?

A westbound phalanx of U.S. Army helicopters passes over sparkling palm fronds, pearlescent pimp wagons, you name it.

Netherworld, Cui says, here we come.

We've been living on the river for days now, in the shadow of a vaulted overpass. A pair of nesting peregrines fills the ironwork with their vigilance. The traffic roar is constant, the one falcon's stare never falters.

At night from water's edge comes the gleam of other eyes: cat, dog, possum, human. One night we see a lost-looking coyote. It approaches the river sideways on mincing furtive steps, looks around, lowers its snout to lap.

Cui eases open the broken zipper on the sleeping bag.

Trickster nation, he says, and sidles down the slanting concrete.

The coyote is long gone by now. In its place lies Cui, belly down and spread-eagle, tattooed lips dipping into the current.

Taste it, he says, offering his cupped, dripping hands.

I close my eyes and sip the darkness from his reflection.

Once, when I was little, I hid a penny in my mouth. I was telling my parents a lie. Though at the time I got away with it, the price I still pay persists in the galvanic bitterness that shocks me awake from certain dreams.

In one of these dreams the river is sweeter than that penny but just as flat and hard and cold on my tongue, and Cui, though I can hear him, is invisible.

The Ganges, his voice is saying, We forgot to say the Ganges.

I am using a charred wooden pole to turn bones on a blazing funeral pyre. But this is not that dream. I am not sleeping.

One steaming summer night Cui comes home from a construction-site raid with a waxy-looking lump in a vial of water. He unstops the cork, holds it smiling to my lip.

Hmm, I say. Garlic? Smells good.

Sure it does, Cui says, my favorite silly girl. And flings it across my face.

It feels cold then hot and for a second I want to smile back, though I'm no longer sure he was really smiling; and then my cheek is on fire, burning, peeling off in smoking strips that blister and pop on the faded mural where we have scraped each other raw making love.

I throw myself into the river.

Underwater through my hair I see a greenish-golden glow and when I come up gasping Cui pitches the vial at my head.

A snaky line of flame erupts on the water's surface and Cui is yelling, Calm down, beautiful! I'm gonna save you! Calm down!

But when he jumps in to grab me, I claw my way to the other side and keep running even after he falls to his bony knees in the muck.

He's yelling Don't do this to me, you'll regret it, you'll see!

In the night air my naked jawbone sizzles.

White phosphorus is what they tell me at the Emergency. Exposed to air, burns even when re-submerged in water. Known historically as napalm, a once-popular item in the Dow Chemical family of products. Still used in rat poison, fertilizers, black-market fireworks, etc. Scars keloid if you're like me and my fair-skinned family.

My family refrains from questioning the choices I made in my state, as they phrase it, even as they thank God for the safe return of their daughter. This goes on for a while. When the nurse stops coming to change my dressings they give me this leather-bound sketchbook and some pencils. The sketchbook has gilt edges, a silk ribbon, and Bible-story engravings by Gustave Doré, these otherworldly chiaroscuros I remember from before meeting Cui hanging out by the Art Building fountain and running off with him to be free. The fucker.

And yet some nights before falling asleep I turn a page. The pencil starts moving, and instead of Cui rotting away in prison or burning in hell, the way I know he should be, there we are again, flying over the desert, floating down by the river, as if all we ever wanted were the wings.

THE PAPER MAN

DUPREE'S LAST CAST was perfect. The handtied fly seemed to hang in the twilight for a long and brilliant second before floating down to kiss the surface of the water. He had finally hit the smallest ring at the pool's far end. If only he could cast like that up on the river, where presentation really counted, instead of here, in his freshly chlorinated swimming pool. Still, it was one way to end a vacation, better than some he could imagine. He reeled in the line, propped his rod against the patio bar, and picked up the flexible bottle of charcoal lighter fluid. He was about to douse the stacked briquettes when Jennifer called from the kitchen window.

Someone was knocking, she said—knocking hard—at the living room door.

"Can't you get it?" Dupree answered. "My hands are full of soot."

"Well, mine are full of fat," Jennifer said.

She held up the chicken she was skinning. It emitted a naked, pearly sheen. Though it was nearly September there were June bugs on the sill. Dupree took aim at the briquettes and gave the bottle a squeeze.

"Who is it?" he asked. The chicken vanished from his view.

"I'm sure I don't know," Jennifer said.

"I'll bet I do," Dupree said. "How much you want to bet?"

"Well, go and see then. Maybe it's the Bosch guy, if we're lucky."

"The what guy?"

"The guy from Bosch."

"I thought they already fixed the washing machine."

"They did," Jennifer said, "except now it tears up everything on Delicate."

Dupree put the lighter fluid down and made as if to dust the soot from his hands. His hands were not really full of soot. He had used tongs to erect his little charcoal pyramid.

"Richard, please," Jennifer pleaded. "They're knocking."

The first bat of the coming evening flickered over the pool and disappeared. Dupree drank off his vodka, smelling lighter fluid on his hands.

"I'll bet it's those religious fanatics again," he said. "They're overdue."

Dupree crossed the patio and entered the service porch, which led into the kitchen. The chicken skin was like a glove on Jennifer's hand. She swung her eyebrows toward the living room, where harpsichords played softly over the classical station. The knocking stopped and started again.

"Well, if it is who you think it is, don't go getting into it with them again," Jennifer said.

"Save me the liver," Dupree said.

"Because they positively thrive on people like you."

"And the heart. I get the heart."

"*Cholesterol,*" Jennifer sang. "Just get the door."

But when Dupree turned on the porch light and opened the door, it was not to the urgent couple he had learned to expect. The man standing there, in fact, bore no overt signs of the evangelical, he had no pamphlets, no clip-on necktie, no black valise. He was a fat man, very fat, and he stood there combing fat fingers through his hair, which was graying and long enough to hide his collar. He glanced from Dupree out toward the street, where a dusky station wagon idled at the curb. Dupree had the feeling he had seen the station wagon before, but not the man, who smelled of ointment.

"Yes?" Dupree said.

"You don't know me, Mister Dupree," the fat man whispered.

Dupree kept his hand on the edge of the door. He did not like to be addressed that way by strangers who had no business knowing his name, not since a certain personal injury case he had litigated the year before. The case was the result of a neighborhood feud that had steadily escalated, from garbage can raids and front lawn fires to crude surveillance and mistaken identity, until the mistaken party got his fingers slammed and crushed in his own car door. The case was an ugly one and when Dupree had won it he went through a time thinking the defendant might be crazy enough to send someone after him to do bodily harm.

"That's right," Dupree said. "I don't know you."

The fat man took a breath and his shirt ballooned. Dupree saw that the print worked into the cloth—weeds and bugs and fish and frogs and birds and larger predators—was meant to illustrate, in a sporting sense, the natural food chain.

"And I don't know you, Mister Dupree. I know your name, but I don't know how you're going to respond."

"Respond to what?" Dupree asked.

"To the question my father made me promise I would come up here and finally ask you."

Dupree let go of the door. He had known it all along. Valise or no valise, the man was a fanatic.

"Listen," Dupree said, relishing the lie he was about to tell. It was the same lie he always told these front porch prophets. "We're Catholics here. We *like* the pope."

He crossed his arms and waited for a reaction. They usually launched right in at that, reciting dire Bible verses and pointing. But all the fat man did was smile and look relieved.

"I'm glad to hear that, Mister Dupree," the fat man whispered. "Because so am I, and so is my father. My name is Rudy. Rudy Llewellyn."

The name sounded vaguely familiar, though Dupree couldn't seem to place it.

"*Is* it the Bosch man?" Jennifer called from inside the kitchen.

"I'm with the morning *Herald*," the fat man whispered.

It took a second for that to register. "Oh, the paper," Dupree said. "But we already subscribe."

"I know you do," the fat man said. He was sweating great beads of sweat in the moth-proof porch light. The moths were out there anyway, batting their yellow wings. "I deliver it to you every morning, daily and Sunday."

So that was why the station wagon looked familiar; Dupree was an early riser. "Then, what's your question?" he asked, quite sure he didn't want to hear it.

"Mister Dupree, I'm here to ask a favor for a dying man."

Jennifer came into the living room drying her hands on a paper towel. Dupree could see her nostrils quiver slightly at the ointment smell.

"Who is it?" she asked.

Dupree said, "The paper man. The morning *Herald*."

74

Jennifer did not hesitate. "I already paid that bill," she said, peering over Dupree's shoulder. "I pay online, every month, on the dot."

Rudy nodded and glanced back out at the station wagon. Dupree could see white exhaust in the waning light.

"Mister Dupree—Mrs. Dupree—I know this is going to sound strange, but my father used to live here. Right here in this very house. He lived here with my mother, before I was born—and I'm fifty-six." He seemed embarrassed to mention his age. "Anyway, it was a long time ago."

Dupree felt Jennifer's hand in the small of his back. He could tell what she was thinking by the way she pressed. *Close the door. He might be crazy. Close the door.*

"Well?" Dupree asked.

"My father's out there waiting right now in the car. I know how this must sound, but he'd like you to let him come in. He wants to come in, I don't know, and look around."

His whisper was full of catches. The curving line of streetlights blinked on and off, and then stayed on.

"Believe me," the fat man said. "I wouldn't ask if he wasn't dying."

Dupree looked out at the station wagon again. There was no one in it that he could see.

"I'm afraid not," Jennifer said. "You tell him, Richard. Not tonight."

She pressed her fingers into the small of his back.

Dupree said, "I'm afraid that—"

"It would just be for a minute," Rudy interrupted. "Just so he could take one last look around."

"Richard, tell him we're busy and shut the door."

"Wait a second," Rudy said. His shoulders were heaving. He mopped his brow. "You're worried I'm lying. You maybe think

75

I'm making this whole thing up. You're not even sure I'm really the guy who delivers your paper. But listen to this. You just got back from ten days' vacation. You stopped delivery on the seventeenth—that was a Sunday—and you started up again yesterday, right? You send me fifty dollars every Christmas, which I hope you know I appreciate. And the only paper you ever missed since I've been running this route was back in May. Three months ago. The day of the exploratory. They took one look and sewed him back up, just like that. This kid, he took my place, it was only for a day, but he ended up missing just about every address he could. Forty-two complaints. Don't think I didn't hear about it, because I did. But me, I hit your driveway, near the gate here—right about here. And when it rains I always porch it. Isn't that the truth?"

When the man finally finished, his face was drenched. He stood there waiting to be called a liar. Jennifer's hand went away from Dupree's back. The harpsichords modulated.

Dupree cleared his throat. "He just wants to look around?"

"It's all he talks about the last month and a half."

"Richard," Jennifer said.

"Five minutes," Rudy was saying. He was no longer weeping but his eyes were red. "Five minutes and we'll be gone. I give you my word."

He stood there waiting for an answer, but before Dupree could offer one, the passenger door of the station wagon eased open from the inside, and the figure of a very old man in a sagging bathrobe inched slowly out. He emerged slippers first, as if he had been lying on his back, and stood up tentatively on the strip of grass. His whole attention seemed to be focused on the effort of standing. Rudy looked back and forth. He wrung his hands and shifted his weight and then he hurried down the brick walkway, hitching his pants and breathing heavily as he went.

Jennifer said, "If you need me, I'll be in the kitchen, dialing 911."

"Take it easy," Dupree said.

"And what if he dies in here? Then what?"

"Nobody's going to die."

"Get it in writing," Jennifer said. "You're the lawyer who reads the obituaries. You know the risks."

Jennifer went back into the kitchen. Water started running fast in the sink. Dupree watched as Rudy leaned in the driver's window of the station wagon and turned off the engine, then came back around to the old man's side and put his arm around his waist. They were making their way back up the steps to the front door.

"Dad, this is Mister Dupree," Rudy managed to pant when they got close. "Mister Dupree, this is my father, Mister Llewellyn. I told him we can't take but five minutes of your time. He understands."

The old man was gaunt and yellow-skinned and his hair hung in patches on his skull, but there could be no doubt about the relation. They were father and son. The old man looked at Dupree and said, "Thank you, Mister Dupree. You're an understanding man." From the kitchen came the sound of the food processor shredding something.

Dupree stepped away from the door and said, "Five minutes."

Once inside, the old man's face seemed to absorb the lamp light. His head pivoted stiffly from side to side, but his eyes were clear and quick. Dupree thought he must be looking for something familiar, some kind of reminder. Rudy kept his arm around his father's waist. His shirt was brilliant beside the limp brown robe. They were both wearing the same brown quilted slippers, crushed down at the heels.

Dupree finally broke the silence. "We, uh, did most of the renovation ourselves," he said. The water had stopped running. Jennifer would be listening as well as she could. "The hardwood floors. The slate hearth there. Knocking out the wall just where you're standing. Why, there's six months of weekends in all that molding if there's a day."

Neither Rudy nor Rudy's father offered any response. The two-minute hourly news came on the radio. Missiles were being redeployed. Floodwaters were rising steadily. The old man's mouth worked as if trying to match the announcer's words. The three of them stood on the oak parquet listening to the rapid-fire capsule bulletins. A national forest was burning out of control. The Dow was up. At the mention of American League action tonight the old man removed his son's vast arm from around his waist.

He said, "I would like to see the nursery, if I may."

"The nursery?" Dupree said.

"We had a nursery. It faced the garden."

"Oh," Dupree said, "you mean my workshop. The realtor said that was the maid's room when we bought."

"If it faces the garden, it was the nursery."

"It faces the pool now. The swimming pool."

"Dad?" Rudy said.

"I'm fine," the old man said. He took a careful step, and then another. "It's down the hall, if I remember, Mister Dupree."

Dupree was beginning to feel the strain of being called Mister Dupree by two men old enough to be his father and his grandfather. Not even his secretary called him that. Only judges did.

"That's the way, all right," Dupree said, feeling less and less like the deeded property owner. "It gets pretty dark in that hall past sundown though. There. *Fiat lux.*"

Dupree took his hand away from the light switch and felt suddenly giddy. He found himself following the old man down the hall, past framed family portraits, past the thermostat. He had never walked down any hall so slowly before. He realized that Rudy was staying behind, was just going to stand there in the living room with the classical music. The old man's slippers shuffled on the apricot runner like dry skin chafing.

"There's not much to see, to tell the truth," Dupree said. "I'm getting new paneling pretty soon."

He was talking to keep from hearing the sound of those slippers. They never really lifted clear of the runner, and the shuffling sound was constant. Under the robe Dupree could see the bony shapes of the old man's shoulder blades. When the old man stopped at the end of the hall Dupree made quick to lean forward and push open the door. He flicked on the light over his fly-tying bench and then stepped back to let the old man enter before him, one shuffling step at a time.

Inside, the old man peered before him as if hearing something Dupree couldn't. The kitchen sounds had stopped and the music didn't reach back this far in the house. Again Dupree felt obliged to break the deepening silence.

"Did you ever try fly fishing?" It was the only question that came to mind. "My firm rents this wild trout stream up in Idaho every year. We just got back."

But the old man wasn't listening. He was gazing out the window.

"We had a garden," the old man said. "Nothing fancy, you understand. Mostly roses, and a lemon tree. But the scent would sift in here on summer nights."

As he spoke, he picked up a pair of needle nose pliers from among Dupree's fly-tying paraphernalia. The steel was blue in his yellowed fingers. His nails were long.

"We were lonely, my wife and I, that is, until Rudy came along. I used to come in here and watch him sleep when he was young." He worked the pliers back and forth. "You don't have any children of your own, do you, Mister Dupree?"

The ointment smell had gathered as if in a knot about the folds of his robe. Dupree's stomach was about to turn. He shook his head.

"Some people prefer it that way, I know. But we had Rudy."

He replaced the pliers on the bench amidst the colored threads and fur and feathers.

"Thank God you're Catholic," the old man said. "Rudy told me when he came to help. You waste your talents, you kill your wife, you have confession."

But he didn't get to talk anymore about that, for Rudy's shirt appeared in the window, its design reflected back in dark reverse. Rudy said, "Come on now, Dad. Let's go. Mister Dupree's been more than generous."

Rudy guided his father back to the front door, thanking Dupree over and over, and promising that he could always count on Rudy Llewellyn to deliver the news. Dupree waited for the station wagon's taillights to round the curve before carefully closing and locking the door; and then he found himself just as carefully unclenching his fist. It was his casting hand, the hand he worked the tongs with, and it was hot and white and trembling. The giblets were sizzling. The plumbing rumbled.

"This is a test," said a voice on the radio.

"Only a test," Dupree heard himself say.

THRESHOLD

AT FIRST I THINK it's the soft-core channel, this flat sort of in-and-out panting. It's waking me up on the couch. I'm sweating and beery and it's Friday night, late. I'd just as soon keep on snoozing.

I've dozed off watching some kind of ballerina skit. This creamy centerfold was lacing up her toe shoes. I remember her bent from the waist knotting black satin ribbons. She was watching herself watch herself in a wall mirror. I figure by now she must be into the heavy breath finale, which is what's waking me up in the first place. I open my eyes and blink.

The television set isn't even on. All I can see of it is this gleam, like a smile or a knife in the dark. But I still hear that fast shallow breathing. I roll over onto my side and listen harder.

It comes to me from inside the kitchen. My head is clearing, I'm awake now. What the hell is going on? I get up and move toward the sound.

My wife starts when she sees me in the doorway. She stands there barefoot on the linoleum in the little light from her sewing machine. She's gulping mouthfuls of hot August air. Her arms hug her nightgown around her high swollen belly. She looks scared and more pregnant than ever.

"What?" I ask. She keeps breathing that way. "Honey, what's the matter? What is it?"

"A man," she finally manages to say.

"A man," I say, "what about a man?" But she can't breathe to speak. I say, "Where?" three different times.

She swallows hard enough finally to catch half a breath. "In the window," she says, "the door window." She says this without looking at the glass. "I looked up from my sewing and he was standing there. Just standing there, staring in." She shudders up and down her long body, which the baby inside has bloated. "He had something in his hand. Something shiny."

I hold her, smooth her hair. I try to soothe her. Behind her the two of us are reflected in the window. For a second I wonder if she isn't just seeing things. But she's shaking hard now, deep from inside. I push my eyes through our reflection in the glass.

Out back nothing stirs in the moonlight. I scan for any movement but even the wind chimes hang still. Whoever was out there will be long gone by now.

We reappear in the glass. I notice a crack in one corner I've never noticed before. My wife's trembling begins to subside. On the table beside us her Singer idles warmly. It makes an up-and-down humming sound. Its hooded light shines down on a jumble of red cloth, on an unfinished stitch in the material.

"Awful late to be up still sewing, don't you think?"

"I couldn't get to sleep in this heat."

"Maybe now. Maybe now you can get to sleep."

She stiffens. "Not now."

"Don't worry. I'll be right in."

"What are you going to do?"

"Check around a little is all. Make sure everything's like it should be."

She leans back and looks at me closely. "It isn't," she says. "It's not."

"Well I just want to make sure for myself. Okay?"

"You won't go out there, will you? Will you?"

"Not if you don't want me to I won't."

"No," she says. "It's not safe to go out there."

"I won't then, okay? Come on."

Her shoulders rise and then drop and stay dropped.

"Will you call the police?"

"I'll call them. Now come on."

I lead her to the bedroom and get her into bed. Then I go through the house switching on lights. I lock all the windows and deadbolt the doors and wish we could afford central air. In this heat wave we're having it's going to get hot, but there's not a whole lot else I can do. I'd rather sweat than have her get overstressed. I double-check every lock, latch and chain, then I pick up the telephone.

I don't want to make a big deal out of dialing Emergency. The less excitement the better, I figure. So I look in the phone book and call the main police business number and give the switchboard our name and address. The main thing, they tell me, is remember to stay calm at all times. I hang up and take a last look around. I'm calm enough, no problem, but I'm worried about my wife. It's been a rough seven months already. My wife is high-strung, which is not good when you're pregnant, especially if you're over thirty-five. My wife will be thirty-eight here pretty quick. In the kitchen I uncap a half gallon of Rhine wine and take it and two water glasses into the bedroom.

"Still awake?" I want her to see me smiling.

"What did they say? The police?"

"They said not to worry. They're sending a squad car right out."

She looks from me to the two glasses up to me again. I set the bottle and one glass down on the nightstand and close her fingers around the other one.

"A little nightcap," I say.

"I can't," she says. But she wants it. I can see.

"One little glass of wine's not going to hurt."

"But—"

"Baloney. Calm you down. Doctor's orders." I clink glasses and wait for her to take the first sip. Finally she wets her lips some and swallows.

"You're sure it's okay?"

"Of course I'm sure." I just want her to calm down and go to sleep. After wetting her lips like that a couple more times, she leans back on the pillow and takes a deep breath. This is an encouraging sign.

We sit up in bed then sipping and waiting and not talking much. There's really not much to say. The obvious thing that we both avoid mentioning is that my wife has good reason to be afraid. She knows what it feels like to be broken in on. It happened to her just before we got married. When she called me she could hardly talk, and once I got over to her apartment I saw why. I made sure she didn't look in any mirrors and got her to the hospital as fast as I could. Her life was never in serious danger but it took the plastic surgeons hours to put her face back together. They did an amazing job, they really did, and now I'm the only one who can see through it when she smiles.

"Cheers," I say when I see her start to fidget.

"It's been nearly twenty minutes."

"It's the weekend," I tell her. "Busy night for the police. Give them a little more time."

"But you said they'd be here right away."

"Nothing's going to happen. Trust me, okay?"

"But what if they got the address wrong? What if they're on the wrong block?"

"They're the *police*," I say, and I hear my voice rise. "Believe me, nothing is going to happen."

We both drain our glasses at the same time. My wife fills hers close to the top, then mine. She's not just sipping anymore.

"I'm sorry," I say. "I'll call them again, okay?" I have to keep calm for both of us.

I get up and go into the living room. With the lights all blazing and no cross-ventilation, the whole house is turning into an oven. The air smells second-hand, like the air inside a balloon. I wish the cops would arrive and put an end to it.

I come back into the bedroom carrying the phone book with one hand and untangling the extension cord with the other. My wife's glass is half empty again.

"This heat," she says.

"Is that any better?" I fold up the blanket, squaring corners.

"Maybe if you tell them I'm expecting," she says. "It can't hurt if you just tell them that."

"Right," I say, and this time I dial the Crime Report number, which is listed just under 911. I want to avoid all the sirens and the lights and all that. I count twenty-six rings before anybody answers. I'm just starting to explain things when a voice in the background says something about "in-progress hostage" something-something. The guy who answered says, "I'm putting you on hold. Don't hang up."

"Well?" my wife says.

"They put me on hold."

I watch her take a deep shaky breath. She lifts the open paperback off the nightstand and right away she's turning pages. I pour us each a fresh glass of wine. My wife fans herself with the book then keeps turning pages.

After a while I start to wonder if I haven't been cut off. But then the desk sergeant comes back on the line. This time he asks me for details.

"My wife was in the kitchen," I say. "She was sewing. Not showing. *Sewing*. Right. She looked up and saw this guy in the window. She's almost positive he had some kind of weapon."

"Something shiny," my wife says.

"Something shiny," I say.

"Shiny," the sergeant repeats. I wonder if he's writing this all down. "Almost positive. Uh huh. What else?"

But then without warning I'm suddenly transferred, about five different times in a row. Each connection sounds farther and farther away until finally I can't hear anything. A recording comes on, with music.

"Now I'm stuck back on hold again."

This time my wife doesn't respond. I watch her turning pages even faster than usual, which is as fast as I've ever seen anybody read. Ever since the assault, and it's been several years, she's read grocery store gore novels just as fast as she can buy them. That and the sewing, it's either one or the other. It's something compulsive, I think. Picture frames, car covers, comforters, shirts—one time she even sewed me a suit. But now she's buried herself inside another book.

The cover on this one shows a thorny red rose with a black dagger sticking through it. Blood drips on the block-lettered title. She's read in some column about the therapeutic value of identifying with fictitious victims. It's always a woman in jeopardy. In these books the bad guys always get caught.

Rapists, mass murderers, rampaging psychos, they're always brought to final fictitious justice. In my wife's case, which was real, they never even brought in a suspect. But she's turning the pages now way too fast, as if she knows the story without having to read.

She does a good quarter inch of book and between us we do three or four inches of wine from the bottle while I sit there with the receiver to my ear. Finally another voice says hello.

It's a woman, I think, though I can't really tell. The connection has gone all gravelly. She starts by informing me that on a night like tonight the department is forced to prioritize. Naturally, I say. I can understand that. I want to remain calm and in control. What with a major incident underway on the other side of town, she says, Peeping Tom calls rank pretty far down the list. I see, I say, working to contain myself, and then she asks if we've considered the advantages of owning our own watchdog, as opposed to installing ornamental grillwork on the windows. Ornamental grillwork, she explains, poses certain life-and-death hazards in the event of a fire scenario, whereas a dog can be taught almost anything. I can't believe this is going on. *Listen,* I want to say, *my wife is jittery enough as it is without an attack dog chained up in the back yard.* But this woman keeps on about how the county pound is giving them away, watchdogs, that is, free, shots and all, for the taking. I thank her for the tip and hang up.

I look at the alarm clock. It's been almost forty-five minutes now. I realize my wife must be feeling the wine. She has put down the paperback and undone her nightgown underneath the designer sheet, and now she's playing grab-ass and nearly crying at the same time. This is not what I wanted. Her stomach makes a mountain of flowers.

"They'll be right here," I say. I look just past her eyes when I say it. I can't let her worry too much.

She lets go with both hands. "That's what you said before."

"Listen," I say. "Just try and relax."

"How can I *relax*? Tell me. How *can* I?"

She pours herself another glass of the wine. I know now the wine was a mistake. She takes a long drink and stares straight at the window shade.

"You think I'm paranoid, don't you? You think I'm just seeing things."

"Get off it," I say. "Of course I don't." I drink off the last of my own glass.

"Then what are you thinking? Hel-*lo*?

"I think maybe we've had enough."

She runs the back of her hand across her forehead. It's like she's aiming for something else. "Maybe we've had enough what?"

Why doesn't she just fall asleep? I spill a little wine pouring myself another.

"Enough wine," I say. "Maybe we've had enough wine."

Until now she's been holding back tears. Now her eyes turn narrow and dry. "Don't you dare," she says. "Don't you dare say another word." She sets her glass down next to the book. "You're the one who brought it in here in the first place."

She's right. What can I say? That I'm afraid of swollen brains, crooked spines, shriveled hearts? We've been through that before, the medical evidence, the link between drinking and birth defects. And besides, that's not what I'm worried about now. I'm worried about her slipping away somewhere I won't be able to reach. That's what I'm worried about. I think, Pull her up out of that hole.

So I say, "What are you sewing in there?"

She looks at me for five separate seconds. I take her hand and trace the veins in her wrist. She lets me do that, barely.

"Pajamas," she says.

"Pajamas?" I say. Her hand gives just the slightest bit.

"For the baby," she says. I keep tracing veins. "I got this Simplicity pattern down at the mall."

"You and your Simplicity patterns," I say. "We're going to have the best-dressed kid on the block."

"Stop it," she says. "You don't have to say that."

"I mean it. I really do."

For a moment we lie there, nearly back with each other. Her hand finally presses back against mine.

"They're going to be darling," she says. "Just wait. Fire-engine red napped flannel, with little feet and a rabbit appliqué."

"A rabbit?" I say.

"Why—what's wrong with a rabbit?"

"I can't think of any rabbit jokes. That's what."

"Be serious now. It's not funny."

"But a *duck*." I knock ashes from an imaginary cigar. "And you say *viaduct*."

A sharp rattling sound wipes the smile from her face. The rattling does not stop and then it stops and starts again.

"Viaduct," she whispers. Her hand closes tighter. I don't want her to see I'm afraid.

"Why a duck?" I say, and I'm straining to hear while she's tensing up all over again, her knuckles, the tendons in the back of her neck. The rattling gets louder and stops.

My wife reaches for the wine but jerks back her hand as if it's touched an invisible wire. "Somebody's out there, I know it." She's wringing my fingers in hers. "They're out there looking in this minute."

I can't let her see it's getting to me too. "But what did I just tell you?" I say. "What did I just finish saying?" She seems to be growing smaller. "Didn't I just finish telling you the police are going to be here any minute now? Well? Didn't I?"

"Don't," she says quietly. "I heard you the first time."

"But isn't that what I just finished saying?"

"I'm afraid they're going to try and get in."

"Who—the police?"

"Stop now."

"But I'm telling you. There's nobody even out there." She's shrinking. "There can't be. It's simple. Will you listen to me?"

"I can feel it," she says.

"Then goddammit let them try and get in. Okay? All right? Let them try and get in and *then* we'll see."

"Shush now. They're out there. They're listening."

That's as far as I can let her go. One step further and I'll lose her again. I reach over and hand her her glass. I don't know what else to do.

"Go ahead," I say. "It's the low-cal stuff. Help you calm down, relax. Go ahead."

She rubs her forehead, the corners of her eyes. Her face is splotchy, the skin almost transparent. She takes the glass in both hands and drinks it down. I pour her another and it's the same thing again, like water, and I pour her the last of the bottle. She drinks that and we sit there in the quiet.

"Okay," I say when I see her eyes start to slide. "Let's think of some names why don't we."

"Names," she says. Her voice is thick at the edges.

"For the baby, you know." Naming names is like hypnotism. "We haven't thought of any names for a long time."

Her eyes drift to the window, then back to me. The shade is pale with moonlight. It's hotter than it's been all night.

"Okay," she says finally. "Boy or girl?"

"Whatever you feel like picking." I'm trying to listen for anything strange. She looks at me as if she can see straight through. Her eyes are floating, unfocused.

"I said girl," she says.

"Girl then, fine. Go ahead. You start." I can't hear a goddamn thing.

"Amelia," she says. We start naming names. We've done this dozens of times. Now we don't bother to argue one over the other. We just recite them back and forth, just the names. Rebecca. Ramona. Veronica. Katherine. Adrienne. Alicia. Nadine. We say each name twice. First she says it, then I say it back. Then she stops and just listens to me. Judy. Jeannie. Jody. Joan. I listen to the spaces in between. I slow down my delivery, make the silences longer. My wife doesn't seem to notice. "Susie," I say. "Sally. Susie. Sally." Her eyes are still half-open. I touch her throat, feel her pulse. She's finally dropped off to sleep.

It's been driving me crazy, the waiting. I get up off the bed, slip out of the room. I go through the house checking windows again. Then I throw open every cupboard and closet. I look in the shower stall and I get down on my knees to look under the couch and when I find myself rifling through the dirty clothes hamper I figure I must be about half-drunk myself. All those Friday night beers, and then the wine on top of that. The whole night seems like something I've dreamed.

I lean on the cool bath tiles for a minute. After a while I notice this line of black ants. They're traveling along the groove of white caulking on the wall. They're going from the windowsill to a crack in the caulking just next to the sink, then disappearing into this crack. The sink, I mean the *faucet* is dripping. I look a little closer at the ants. For some reason they fascinate me. At first I can't figure it out.

Then it hits me. This one line of ants is moving both ways at once. It's going back and forth at the same goddamn time. I have to concentrate to make out the order, but it's there all right—the ants have it. I'm amazed at their ingenuity. Without thinking I reach under the sink and pull out the big red pipe wrench.

I think, If anybody's out there I'll beat them on the head and drag them halfway in through the sliding glass door. As long as they're inside the house you can legally kill them. The wrench makes my arm muscles flex.

First I look in on my wife. She's asleep on her back with her eyes still rolled upward. The sheets contour her big rolling curves. I leave the door open and float into the living room, through the kitchen and into the pantry, where the garage butts up to the house. I go through the garage and out the side door and step outside where I promised I wouldn't go.

The moon is up, hard-edged on one side. For a minute I stand still in its light. I measure my eyes, get used to the depth. Distant traffic sounds make it seem quiet. I take a deep breath, five or six times. What I smell runs from bagged trash to jasmine. A breeze rises and dies on the back of my neck and I realize how hard I am sweating. Then I begin to make out the shadows—trellis skeletons, hanging plants, the line of lawn deer. I shoulder the wrench and start walking.

I'm barefoot as I glide across thick spongy Bermuda. I keep my eyes locked straight ahead. But as the range of my vision extends itself outward, I see nothing more dangerous than the barbeque. A nest of old tennis balls clusters in the moonlight. The garden hose coils in place. I pace off the flowerbeds where my wife weeds every day but there's nobody there, at least not in the open. I heft the wrench and work around toward the dark side of the house.

At the corner of the house I pause for a moment, then step carefully from moonlight into shadow. I step forward, not thinking, no longer even afraid, just staring and moving ahead. The first window I come to is our bedroom.

Through the backlit vinyl shade I can see my wife's silhouette. She sleeps there quietly on the bed. The breaths she takes now are silent stomach-swelling sighs. When she exhales, I can almost feel them rise. I stand still watching her, matching her breathing, and think Jesus, who else would I be doing this for. That's my wife in there. That's the woman I married. When she turns over I can smell her warm vanilla smell in my shirt, as if I was still on the bed there beside her. I take another breath and catch a sharp edge of spilled wine and what I hear then makes me swing with the wrench.

What I swing at isn't there though and I'm pulled forward with the weight to where the sound that I aimed for is coming from. It's this humming sound but it doesn't sound human. It keeps humming, low and steady, just a tone. I lean toward it and it gets louder with every step in the soft topsoil until I'm peering into the cracked kitchen-door window at the Singer on the table, still idling.

Now my own breath is choppy and short, like my wife's was when I first found her in there. I stand still for a minute inhaling the scent of roses and calming down. The little light on the sewing machine shines down on the red flannel. I can see about a half inch of space between the needle and the color. The needle vibrates in place with the electric humming, and I think of that line of ants. They must have secret signals or something.

After a time I can almost see my wife in the kitchen there sewing. I know she's in the bedroom, on the other side of the

93

wall, but I can see how she would sit there at the machine. She would press the lever under the table with the side of her knee and bend over to guide the material. She would guide it in a curve around the up-and-down blur of the needle. The pressure in her knee would control the needle's speed, and I can feel that pressure now in my own knee. I can feel the hum in my hands and see the pajamas taking shape, though I know that none of this is true as I stand here. I know that none of it is true and yet I see it so clearly that when she slips I feel the needle pierce my own nail. I am pinned to the material, inside her aching body, and when she looks up at the window I am blinded.

A voice says, "Drop it or you're dead. Police."

I stumble.

"*Now.*"

The wrench thumps down underneath the rose bush.

"Now put your hands on your head. Now sit."

He lets me see his gun in the torch beam in front of him. I sit down hard in the dirt. I wonder if maybe he hasn't clubbed me.

"This is a mistake," I say. I can't see through the light.

"Keep your hands on your head. Some i.d."

"But I'm the guy who called you in the first place. I live here."

"You were looking inside that window."

"Yeah, but there was this guy my wife—"

"Keep your *hands* on your *head.*"

"I'm telling you. He was watching my wife."

"And so you thought you'd come out and see for yourself."

He holds the light aimed straight in my eyes. Then he tips it down and glances in the window. I see that my heel is bleeding from a cut fine enough not to hurt yet. The light shoots back in my eyes.

"There's nobody in there," he says.

"My *wife* is. In the bedroom."

"Then she won't mind coming out to identify you."

Suddenly I feel very sober. "My wife is sick," I say. "She's going to have a baby." Behind the light I hear his handcuffs click. "But sure. Go ahead. Wake her up if you have to. You'll probably have to knock pretty hard."

He doesn't move right away. He stands there pointing his light in my eyes. I hear him take a breath of his own, then he lets the beam fan away across the ground.

"I suppose if it was you I was looking for you wouldn't even be here."

"I wouldn't?" I hear him holstering his gun.

"You can get up," he says. He snaps the flap shut on his holster. "I said you can get up off the ground if you want to."

I hesitate. "Where would I be then?"

"Listen, mister."

"I mean it. Where do you think I would be?"

"How do I know? Home getting your rocks off in a Kleenex. Now get up."

Standing, I have to feel for my balance.

"You know that sewing machine in there's still on," he says. In the ground glow I can see he is not young.

"My wife left it that way," I say.

"So then why don't you go back inside now and shut it off, okay? Before the sun catches you creeping around."

He leaves me standing in the shadow. I look up at the sky. The moon is coming out from behind the eaves. I lean down for the wrench and slice my finger, deep, on something sharp and shining. It's a sliver of glass from the cracked window reflecting the light, and now the blood is running. I leave a trail going back inside.

SINKERS

SPOOKY CAME IN AGAIN slurring his words and finally got his arm crushed in the big drill press. I'd seen it coming for days. The day shift was pissed. "There go the fight tickets," they kept saying. We got the tickets for accident-free man hours. I didn't care much about the fights though just then. Spooky was my partner, so I got off early for a change, since you needed two guys to operate that press, and Spooky's arm was still mostly inside of it. Brand new eighty-dollar tattoo, gone like that. Funny thing was, I had the same one myself. This black panther one. Other arm.

Outside it wasn't even lunch time. I walked across the lot to my car humming through my teeth like the power lines. I figured it was time for a new bandana, or a darker pair of shades. I needed something to kill the time. So I drove around for a while staring pedestrians down. Then I parked and walked along with all the losers. This was downtown, where everybody bunched up at the corners waiting for the light to turn green, then stepped around each other getting across. I could have kicked any one of them and they wouldn't have missed a single step. They didn't know how thirsty I was. I got a Coke with extra ice at that Chicken Boy place and ate the ice walking along down Broadway. My skin felt like it wasn't stuck on right.

At Woolworth's the glass doors were clouded up with handprints. I leaned on the decals with my shoulder and went in. Inside, the air moved around on the back of my neck. The racks were full of two-dollar sunglasses. They all pinched behind my ears or weren't dark enough or looked foolish. I scratched all the lenses on my belt buckle putting them back. Then I got on the escalator and watched my hand on the rubber rail. It went faster than me going down.

Downstairs this girl with straight hair was plucking her eyebrows behind the cash register. She was using a mirror the size of a quarter. I was just about the only guy down there so I pretended to browse around. I checked out the painted turtles in glass dishes all around her. After a while I went up and asked her who painted the turtles. She said she didn't know a thing about that. I said whoever it was must have an awful small paint brush. She thought that was a pretty good one. I could tell she liked talking to me. I'd been working on my triceps at home. I rolled up my sleeve and told her all about Spooky. I showed her where they had to saw the panther in two to get the rest of his arm out. She listened with her eyes wide open. One was bluer than the other one. I picked out two turtles to buy. She put them in this paper carton with a wire handle like the ones they give you for chop suey. I told her she could keep the change. She wouldn't do that, but when I asked she wrote her phone number on the side of the carton. The turtles were scratching around inside. I told her I'd call. She said any time after six. "And don't forget to give them their names."

So I called her the next day and went over. She lived in a pink house on a corner with her kid and her father. All the kid did all day was hang around in the tool shed out back watching the old man melt lead for deep sea sinkers. Neither one of them had much to say. She told me the kid's father was locked up in the prison hospital at Atascadero, for trying to pour the old man's hot lead down her throat. The old man was out to the liquor store when this had almost happened, but he'd come back just in time to grab his claw hammer. He'd used the claw side, she said. It had left these two little holes. The kid's father hadn't come to until way after sundown. She dug her fingernails in my arm when she told me about that, chipped red ones that left marks in the skin.

I started hanging around there when I wasn't at work, eating dinner, spending the night. She did things I'd never had done for me before. She'd bring me coffee while I was shaving, or leave notes in my car. Pretty soon though she wanted me to move in for good. She wanted me home every night. But I wasn't in any hurry to do that. Not with her kid and the old man. I told her I'd have to think.

One night the four of us went out fishing on the barge off Redondo. We had plenty of sinkers, that's for sure. We had round ones, flat ones, long ones, square ones, and these defects like broken noses or something. She packed baloney sandwiches and Fritos and donuts with lots of beer, and grape soda for the kid. The old man caught the first one. He stepped on its head to tear the hook out, then threw it back overboard. "Junk fish," was all he said. The good ones we stuck in a gunny sack. I got sick over the side and then I was okay again and she held onto me underneath the army blanket. The kid disappeared for a while. When he came back he was excited. He said for us to come around to the other side of the deck.

They had this big floodlight over there shining down on the water. Everybody was reeling up tangled lines, all but this one guy whose rod was bent double. The line was pulled tight and it was slicing all over the water. One of the deck hands was leaning over the rail with a long-handled gaff while the skipper aimed down with a shotgun.

The shark finally thrashed to the surface then dove back under the hull. It was a while before the guy worked it back up. When he did the deck hand reached down and got the gaff under the shark's head and flipped it over belly up for the skipper. The belly was white and it exploded with the shots, first yellow, then red, but the shark kept thrashing a while longer. When they hauled it up on board they found a bunch of baby sharks all twisted up inside. The kid picked one up and put it inside our gunny sack.

By the time we got back to the house it was morning. The old man emptied the sack on the brown grass out back. Most of them were bonito and one barracuda, with teeth. He turned on the hose and started cutting. The gut bucket filled up fast. The whole time the kid sat there rolling fish eyes under his finger. She was inside the house taking a shower.

That night the old man passed out on the davenport. The davenport was a real antique. Somebody down the block had supposedly overdosed on it, and they'd gotten it for free just for dragging it away. The old man liked to lay on it and drink beers and smoke cigarettes. But when he woke up this time the davenport was on fire. He rolled around on the rug to put his undershirt out, then he pulled the hose in and made the whole room a mess. She smeared a stick of butter on his chest and put the kid back to bed. I never got to sleep the whole rest of the night.

The last time I went over there she already had a picnic made up. She said a picnic was what the both of us needed. The old man stayed at home. We took the kid along with us. We went out to the frog pond out behind the speedway. You could hear the stock cars pretty loud. It was a Sunday afternoon. The kid said he wanted to fish. She took a bobby pin out of her hair and broke off the plastic tip with her teeth.

"Here's a hook," she said. "And here's some string. I'll bet you can find a good sinker somewhere."

The kid went down to the water and disappeared behind the weeds. We stretched out on the blanket and drank the bottle of wine.

She finally said, "When are you going to move in all the way?"

I didn't want to talk about that. She put her head down on my belly. I could feel the vibrations in her throat when she started humming. The stock cars were going around. I suddenly didn't want to be there. I wanted to be by myself. I was easing her up when we heard the splash.

I ran down there through the weeds. The kid had fallen in the pond. The water was thick and full of lumpy green slime. I waded in and pulled him out. The green stuff was warm. I had to breathe through my mouth to keep from heaving. The kid was screaming and scared. She kept saying, "Baby, don't cry now. You're okay now. Don't cry." I drove them home and said I'd be back for dinner.

But I never went back. I never saw them again. I didn't need that kind of grief all the time. They got me a new partner at work, this biker for Jesus with metal teeth. But at least he stayed away from the downers. I threw the turtles away when they died. For the next couple months they had lots of overtime at work, and I put it in, watching the man hours add back up.

ENGRAVED

THE YEAR YOU WERE BORN I don't think I ever fell asleep before the paper hit the wooden screen door. That was back when they still delivered the *Examiner* in the morning. I'd lay there in that big bed of ours and just worry myself sick about your father. He was already starting to have troubles at work. I'd worry about him and then I'd worry about Nana, if she'd live to see you or not. I'd lay there in that little bedroom with the window wide open just so I could hear the freeway, for company, those nights your father wasn't there. I'd worry about the silliest things, all the babies in limbo, the atom bomb, until the paperboy came down the sidewalk hitting porches and people's screen doors. Then I'd fall off to sleep just sick about things I didn't even know, like how if I worried too much you might feel it there inside me and show it up being born a harelip or something. I was so young.

Your father he was already having troubles. I know I said that already, but he was. He'd come home from the plant and just sit there in the kitchen like some old man. He wouldn't tell me what the matter of it was and he'd fly off the handle if I asked. When I told him what I thought he needed was maybe a hobby, he'd say he already had one. He said he played the violin, but I said that's not what I meant to say. I thought if he took up something a little more modern, since his parents made him play it in the first place. They were straight off the boat, those two. She wouldn't look a cat in the eye, or let two mirrors face opposite each other, out of fear of I never knew what. They made him play that violin, and he could play it too, so sweet, but he hated it and said that no child of his would ever have to do that for him. And then he would go get it from out of the front closet and take it out of its wooden box and just play until I couldn't stand it anymore, those old-country tunes there in the kitchen while I heated up Nana's soup. He'd play it for you there inside of me right up against my belly, and I swear I was so young or so dumb or whatever it was, I thought you'd be able to hear it clean through.

I worked there at Newberry's as long as I could, engraving initials or what not on bracelets and things. I sat in this little booth near the jewelry counter. People would come in and ask could I make them a CLJ, or a PBR or some such, and I'd turn on my little drill and spell it out right there for them in these beautiful flowing letters. It was just a knack I had, I don't know where I got it from, until one day it got so slow I fit my whole name and address on the back of this tiny cross. But then they let me go the next day. They said I was getting too big. They said it was bad for business and how I ought to understand. That's just how things used to work.

So I started staying home making you sweaters and mittens and taking you places I thought might be fun, in case we couldn't afford it when you came, or there was a war on or something. I'd finish knitting one sleeve and then take the bus down to Long Beach and we would ride on the merry-go-round. Then the next day I'd finish the other one, and we would visit the Natural History Museum. Nana could still take care of herself in the days then and your father was holding on at the plant. He'd be OK for weeks at a time.

One day we decided to splurge. Your father read about it in the Sunday paper. I even remember the date. It was September the twenty-third. The Red Cars were still running back then so we took a Red Car out as far as it went and then we walked the last mile to the landing field. I liked to walk and I thought it did me good, no matter what your father's mother tried to say. She said you would come out a clubfoot if I did too much walking, but I refused to believe that, and when we got to where we could see it bobbing up and down there the way it did on those long bending lines, your father said it looked just like me, like I had a little blimp underneath instead of a stolen watermelon, the way people used to always say. The blimp it was tied up there on those lines and they were selling rides for $5 a person. We figured it out for us that it broke down to only three-thirty-three-and-a-third apiece, that's counting you, you see, supposing they didn't have special children's rates, which they didn't. In fact, they weren't even letting children go up at all under twelve, and here we were as good as sneaking you on board in broad daylight, though you weren't even really born yet. We got a kick out of that.

So they locked us up in that little room there underneath the blimp part, us and six other people plus the pilot. The pilot he told a few jokes and then they undid the line and up we went, like a bubble, or a giant balloon, and the ground flattened out and got bigger. Everybody ooh-ed and aah-ed and said There's this and There's that, and Those are lemon groves, not orange, and this one older man said he had flown over the Eiffel Tower in a balloon back when balloons were the only way you could do that. He had a white mustache and a pretty French accent, and spit in my eye if your father didn't start talking to him in French. I never even knew he knew French, but he had a way with him sometimes of just catching you by surprise. Like when he would fix the radio with one of my broken earrings, or eat a whole bowlful of batter before I could bake the darn cakes he was always asking for. That's when he was feeling good of course, and that day up there in the blimp we were both feeling good. He held both my hands in both of his and he would talk a little French and then point out the window at some seagulls or an airplane and for a while there that day with you moving inside me I was so happy I forgot all about the other things.

We passed over the ocean a little and the pilot explained how everything worked, the gas and the propeller and how really much safer we were in a blimp than riding in an elevator even. Then we came back over streets and houses and your father said something to the French man and the French man laughed. I had to ask what he said and he said he had told him how you were already getting your higher education. Everybody laughed at that and I really did feel safe. The butterflies were all gone and your father squeezed my hand and pointed out the window again and said There, you can see our house.

Everybody looked out the window and I looked too and then I could see the French man looking away. He tried to smile some but it didn't come out right, and everybody else was sort of doing the same. Your father went on about all the upkeep expenses and the Italian tiles at the bottom of the swimming pool, and the butler's toupee, and termites. I could feel my face burning but nobody said anything except Is that a fact and You don't mean to say, and when we landed the French man touched my arm and said No thank you when your father invited him over for croquet.

All the way home I felt so bad again, just sick, and neither of us ate any supper. He sat in the kitchen and I went in the bedroom to pray some, but a breeze was blowing the curtains in and out of the freeway sounds, and I couldn't get past the fruit of thy womb. After a while the breeze picked up, and I heard him go into the front closet. He played that violin all night, and when the paper hit the screen door toward dawn he was already gone for work. I must have fallen asleep for once without knowing it, which was strange for how tired I felt, even more tired than usual. But I couldn't go back to sleep.

So I got up and boiled an egg and then I boiled an extra one for you. Then I walked across the project to help Nana with her breakfast and tell her about the blimp trip except for the part that really mattered.

She was so happy to see us just a little bit early and she wanted to feel you kick, but her hands were all numb from the radiation. So she listened instead and said how she couldn't wait to see you. She counted how many more weeks were left on the calendar and asked all about the blimp and then she took out my baby pictures and we looked at them some. She had one old picture of herself as a baby and she fell asleep looking at that one. I put the pictures all away and cleaned up a little and then walked back through the ice plant to our place.

It was a Monday but it felt like a Sunday still with the wind blowing and Nana so sick and your father and all, and you on the way so soon. I didn't know what to do. I turned on the radio but that didn't help and I thought I better do something that would take my mind off of things and maybe cheer me up just a little.

I decided I could bake a nice chocolate cake, from scratch. I put on my apron and went through the cupboards and layed everything out on the sink. I measured the flour and added the oil and beat the eggs and the sugar and the butter. I was melting the chocolate when the telephone rang. It was the plant. They said I better come pick up your father.

I was so worried. The chocolate started burning and I didn't know anything about taking taxis. I put on a sweater and walked over to the boulevard and just started hitchhiking, the way I'd seen sailors do.

This DeSoto pulled over. A man in a blue suit said he would take me anywhere I needed to go. At first I was afraid, but he said it nice like. I got in and he drove me straight over there to the plant and said Good luck when I got out.

There was a gate with a guard in a guard shack. He kind of looked at my apron like, but when I said my name he talked on his telephone and said they were sending somebody right out to fetch me. I remember he said fetch.

This man driving an orange forklift drove out and drove me through all the buildings and big storage tanks and over some railroad tracks near the loading docks. We came to this little wooden building like a tool shed finally, way out back behind the main part of the plant. It had a window too high up to look into. All these men in steel hats were standing around it looking serious when they saw me. One of them said they had just sent for the ambulance. Where is he, I said, is he hurt bad, and the one who had said about the ambulance looked at this other man and he nodded and opened the door.

All of them sort of cleared a path for me then and I crossed myself and then I crossed you and went in. Your father was in there all alone. He was sitting on the floor in the corner sort of hunched up with his hands around his knees. There wasn't any blood I could see right off, and when my eyes got used to the light I could see there wasn't any blood at all. He was just sitting there with his knees up in front of him looking straight ahead, like a statue.

I knelt down on the cement just next to him and said his name. Then I touched him on the cheek with my hand. It was like I could feel all the nerves working under his skin, hot and jumpy. He never moved. He didn't even look when I kissed him, but he was breathing. I could feel he was breathing on my cheek.

The ambulance siren started far off then and came close in a hurry. They had to carry him out of there just like he was, hunched over frozen like that. They gave me his lunch pail and said I could ride to the hospital with him. They didn't say what kind of hospital it was going to be but that didn't matter because you were born inside the hour just fine.

The doctor kept saying how good I did, but that must have been by accident. I was so afraid the whole time, I didn't understand the first thing. I didn't know what I was going to do. I was so young and all I could do was engrave. But I didn't think about that just then. The only thing I could think of was that cake batter there on the sink, how your father liked to clean out the bowl. I'd catch him licking the mixers. But you don't remember him, do you?

CROW

BY THE TIME WE GOT DOWN the mountain to the car, daylight was fading. My head hurt from not eating or drinking. My father hooked a finger through my belt loop and I sprawled on the rocks, drinking from the river. Then he got his rod out from the trunk and started casting.

I stood on the bank watching him cast and retrieve. The line kept tossing farther and farther out. I loved my father but I was hungry and cold and afraid of him, all at once, and then the trout was jumping and shaking water. My father held his rod up to keep the line tight but the trout dived and turned, charging back at him faster than he could reel. The line went slack and when it fouled my father dropped the rod on the rocks and walked into the river, up past his waist, to handline the fish onto the bank.

It was beautiful in his hands, a big shuddering rainbow. He layed it in the grass up off the rocks. It gasped there a few seconds then tried to flip back in the water. My father knuckled it on the head, and again, from the shoulder, until it lay still, gills bleeding, and that wide-open eye black and staring.

"Gorged it," my father said. "But just look at him."

With his pocketknife he snipped the line outside the gaping mouth. There were teeth, and when my father slit the belly a wet, gurgling sound as he peeled out the guts. The guts were purple and filled with a cluster of yellow eggs and the silver spoon with the barbed treble hook. There was nothing to be done about the mess of fouled line. My father cut the tangle out of the reel and tossed it in the willows with the guts and then he built another fire in the black rock circle.

This time the fire was smaller. My father skewered the trout on a stick and held it over the flames until the skin was sizzling and the eyes two hard white BBs. We ate the trout with the leftovers of yesterday's hamburgers and greasy French fries, and though most of it was cold it all tasted good.

When we were nearly finished, two crows appeared on the riverbank. They stood in the waning light studying us, or so it seemed, then hopped toward the willows and started cawing. Soon they were pecking at each other, brandishing wings above their heads and fighting over that string of guts.

My father lifted his arms and made as if to fly at them. The cawing stopped and one crow flew up and disappeared. But the other one stood its ground, getting a grip with its snapping beak then flapping up with those guts to perch high in a burned-out snag. The charred branches were bare and jagged and the trunk was split open where a bolt of lightning must have struck and burned its way in. You could see how the inner wood had died and turned gray.

"You're shaking again," my father said.

He took off his jacket using the sleeves to carry rocks from the fire ring to the car and arrange them on the worn-out floor mats. Then he layed his jacket over my shoulders and lifted me into the front seat and climbed into the back and shut the door.

"Here we go," my father said, though we weren't going anywhere. It was warm inside the dark. I could feel us breathing.

Sometime in the night the cawing started up again. By dawn I was freezing and yet the crow kept on cawing. We got out of the car and were standing by the broken fire ring rubbing our hands over the ashes and still that crow wouldn't stop.

"Ungrateful beggar," my father said.

The crow was still up there on that burned branch. It turned its head toward us and started cawing again, raspy dozens of sore-sounding calls.

"Alright already," my father yelled. "Go find your brother, why don't you?"

He flung a rock that glanced off a lower branch. At the sound the crow crouched and spread its wings and began to lift off but then jerked back and collapsed into itself. Its flight had been arrested and it was flailing, I couldn't tell why, and then it was dangling from the branch, upside down and twisting to get back up on its feet. It was struggling, beating the air and reaching with its open beak and red tongue before finally making it back up on the branch. And then it stood there, this crow, black and cawing.

"Snared himself," my father said.

I looked and saw what he meant. A tangled length of my father's line was snagged in the crow's claws, and now it was caught on the branch of that crooked burned-out tree.

Again the crow tried to lift off and again it was yanked back and hung upside down, twisting, slapping the air, fighting to get back up on the branch. When it succeeded it would stand there tangled up even worse, quiet at first and then cawing, and once more it would try to fly away only to be yanked back down again. After a while it stopped trying and just hung there, glossy and exhausted, neck cocked to gaze down at us.

My father's forehead was full of creases. He looked at me and tried to smile.

"Old pal," he said, "you wait here and don't you move."

I wanted to say No but he was already climbing up the big rock beside the tree. Then he was up on the lowest branch getting his hands and clothes blacker and blacker and stretching his arms up to pull himself higher. He knew how to climb, like a sailor up a ship's mast, and when he got close to the crow it started fighting again, harder, losing feathers and cawing louder. My father reached out with his knife and the crow was a blur around his face as he cut and cut again at the tangled line. It wasn't one strand but many that he had to cut and keep cutting, until the crow was dropping, pulled down by gravity into knowing it was free again to fly, to swoop up toward the treetops into the high dawn sunlight, a sparkling snarl of my father's line trailing behind.

When my father jumped down off the rock his hands and clothes were black from the charred wood of that tree, and his face and neck were scratched raw and red, but he was smiling; and when he picked me up his forehead was smooth again.

"Time to go, old sport," he said.

We took the rocks out of the car and threw them back in the river. With the last one my father said, "Watch."

He reared back and heaved that rock as high as he could. For a second it seemed to hang there, turning against the sky, and when it hit the water going under I thought of all the other trout down there, holding against the current.

But that crow. That crow was going to land in some other tree. It was going to perch there for a while and when it tried to fly away it was going to jerk back and hang up again. It was going to hang there upside down, cawing and swinging in the air, and by then how much farther would we have gone, how many more desperate miles, my father, my dear father and me?

ACKNOWLEDGMENTS

Lasting gratitude for the teachers I was fortunate to have at UCLA—Jascha Kessler, Brian Moore—and in the MFA program at UC Irvine—Oakley Hall, Donald Heiney, William Wiser, Rust Hills, and Joy Williams.

Sincere appreciation and respect to the writers and artists of the Los Angeles Glass Table Collective and What Books Press: Gail Wronsky, Rod Moore, Karen Kevorkian, Chuck Rosenthal, Mona Houghton, and Elena Karina Byrne, with special thanks to Gronk Nicandro for the dreamlike cover art, ash good for the book's design, and Kate Haake for her expert editorial eye.

Warmest thanks to my students who throughout the years have taught me more than I could have hoped for, and my colleagues past and present at CSULB for their example and support: Ray Zepeda, David Fine, Gerry Locklin, Charles Webb, Elliot Fried, Suzanne Greenberg, Lisa Glatt, Bill Mohr, Patty Seyburn, David Hernandez, Alan Rifkin, Robert Guffey, Clint Margrave, Tyler Dilts, Ashton Politanoff, Zara Raheem, and Eileen Klink.

Thanks also to the editors who brought out earlier versions of these stories, especially Andrew Tonkovich of *Santa Monica Review*:

"Terminal Island," *LA Fiction Anthology: Southland Stories by Southland Writers*
"Coming Out Empty," *Southwest Review*

"Isaac Babel," *Santa Monica Review*

"The Lash of Saint Francis," *Santa Monica Review*

"The Paper Man," *The Critic*

"River of Angels," *Santa Monica Review*

"Sinkers," *PEN Syndicated Fiction Project*

"Threshold," *American Fiction*

"Engraved," *The Threepenny Review*

"Crow," *The LBJ: Avian Life, Literary Arts,* and as "Cuervo," translated by Daniel Cooper, in *Párrafo: The Animal Issue*

Finally, to my family—Janet, Lizzy, Daniel, Alison, Pearl, and all the others—endless thanks for the gift of your love.

STEPHEN COOPER, biographer of John Fante and winner of a National Endowment of the Arts grant for his fiction, taught literature, film, and creative writing for many years at California State University, Long Beach and the Writers' Program of UCLA Extension. He lives with his wife in Los Angeles.

WHAT BOOKS PRESS

AN IMPRINT OF

THE GLASS TABLE

COLLECTIVE

LOS ANGELES

WHAT BOOKS feature cover art by Los Angeles painter, printmaker, muralist, and theater and performance artist GRONK. A founding member ASCO, Gronk collaborates with the LA and Sant Fe Operas and the Kronos Quartet. His work is found in the Corcoran, Smithsonian, LACMA, an Riverside Art Museum's Cheech Marin collection

As a small, independent press, we urge our readers to support independent publishers and booksellers. This is easily done by visiting our website, WhatBooksPress.com, where you can purchase books directly from us or from Bookshop.org

2025

Inside the Umber Iris
ERIK MANUEL SOTO
WINNER OF THE GRONK
NICANDRO FIRST BOOK PRIZE
POEMS

Persistence of Singing Woods
JOHN COLBURN
STORIES

River of Angels
STEPHEN COOPER
STORIES

Jukebox
PATTY SEYBURN
POEMS

zirconium ash
JIMMY VEGA
POEMS

It Wasn't Always Like This
JAN WESLEY
POEMS

2024

The Manuscripts
KEVIN ALLARDICE
NOVEL

Father Elegies
STELLA HAYES
POEMS

Slow Return
PAUL LIEBER
POEMS

Dreamer Paradise
DAVID QUIROZ
POEMS

How to Capture Carbon
CAMERON WALKER
STORIES

2023

God in Her Ruffled Dress
LISA B (LISA BERNSTEIN)
POEMS

Figures of Wood
MARÍA PÉREZ-TALAVERA
TRANSLATED BY PAUL FILEV
NOVEL

A Plea for Secular Gods: Elegies
BRYAN D. PRICE
POEMS

Nightfall Marginalia
SARAH MACLAY
POEMS

Romance World
TAMAR PERLA CANTWELL
STORIES

2022

No One Dies in Palmyra Ohio
HENRY ELIZABETH CHRISTOPHER
NOVEL

Us Clumsy Gods
ASH GOOD
POEMS

Skeletal Lights From Afar
FORREST ROTH
FLASH FICTION/PROSE POEMS

That Blue Trickster Time
AMY UYEMATSU
POEMS

2021

Pyre
MAUREEN ALSOP
POEMS

What Falls Away Is Always
KATHARINE HAAKE &
GAIL WRONSKY, EDITORS
ESSAYS

*The Eight Mile
Suspended Carnival*
REBECCA KUDER
NOVEL

Game
M.L. WILLIAMS
POEMS

2020

No, Don't
ELENA KARINA BYRNE
POEMS

One Strange Country
STELLA HAYES
POEMS

*Remembering Dismembrance:
A Critical Compendium*
DANIEL TAKESHI KRAUSE
NOVEL

Keeping Tahoe Blue
ANDREW TONKAVICH
STORIES

2019

Time Crunch
CATHY COLMAN
POEMS

Whole Night Through
L.I. HENLEY
POEMS

Echo Under Story
KATHERINE SILVER
NOVEL

Decoding Sparrows
MARIANO ZARO
POEMS

2018

Interrupted by the Sea
PAUL LIEBER
POEMS

The Headwaters of Nirvana
BILL MOHR
POEMS

WHAT
BOOKS
PRESS

LOS ANGELES